Life of a Savage 3

**Lock Down Publications and
Ca$h
Presents
Life of a Savage 3
A Novel by *Romell Tukes***

Romell Tukes

Lock Down Publications
P.O. Box 944
Stockbridge, Ga 30281
www.lockdownpublications.com

Lock Down Publications
Like our page on Facebook: Lock Down Publications @
www.facebook.com/lockdownpublications.ldp
Cover design and layout by: **Dynasty Cover Me**
Book interior design by: **Shawn Walker**
Edited by: **Mia Rucker**

Stay Connected with Us!

Text **LOCKDOWN** to 22828 to stay up-to-date with new releases, sneak peaks, contests and more…

Thank you!

Submission Guideline.

Submit the first three chapters of your completed manuscript to ldpsubmissions@gmail.com, subject line: Your book's title. The manuscript must be in a .doc file and sent as an attachment. Document should be in Times New Roman, double spaced and in size 12 font. Also, provide your synopsis and full contact information. If sending multiple submissions, they must each be in a separate email.

Have a story but no way to send it electronically? You can still submit to LDP/Ca$h Presents. Send in the first three chapters, written or typed, of your completed manuscript to:

LDP: Submissions Dept
P.O. Box 944
Stockbridge, Ga 30281

DO NOT send original manuscript. Must be a duplicate.

Provide your synopsis and a cover letter containing your full contact information.

Thanks for considering LDP and Ca$h Presents.

Acknowledgements

First and foremost I'd like to thank Allah for blessing me every day and keeping me on my deen. Thank you to all the readers and supporters. I want to give a shout to my family, my brother Sonoke A.K.A Mereno. Shout out Yonkers, NY. we on the build, Shot Fresh, Cb, Awall, PC, YB, Lango, Kuzzy Loc, and Spanghoe. My BX niggas Too Blue, Rico Tramant niggas, B-Robb, Frellz, BJ teh gunner, and to my nigga Trouble East Orange, my D.C niggas Lee, Pacman,Zoe, and Rellz. Philly Big C, and can't forget my son Melly and Roll-out. Thank you to Lockdown for all the support and effort they put into their authors. You can really do anything you put your mind to. Turn your negatives into positive, use your weakness as your strength. Stay awake. There is more to come. We got the game on lock.

Chapter 1
Welcome Home

Miami, FL

Bama woke up in his mini mansion in a cold sweat, as if he was in a cotton field somewhere in the country parts of Alabama.

Lately, since he had been home after his appeal, he had been having nightmares of him killing people and hurting people he'd never seen in his life.

He climbed out of his California king size bed with Paco Rabone sheets. Stepping on his mink rug, his feet sank into the fur. He threw on his Calvin Klein rope and walked into his private bathroom to clean his face with water.

His mini mansion was a gift from Savage. It was 4,121 square feet with four bedrooms, three bathrooms, a four car garage, a bar, and a nice little backyard to throw cookouts in. He also had a living room, dining room, and a huge kitchen.

His master bedroom was the size of six prison cells, with a personal bathroom, walk-in closet full of shoes still in boxes, and designer clothes. There was even a pool table in the middle of his bedroom floor.

After he splashed water on his face, he made wudu and his morning saket (prayer), so he could keep the demons away.

The first week home, Savage bought him two luxury cars and a new wardrobe, as well as appointed him Imam of his mosque because the last Imam moved back to New York.

Bama went by the name Abdulla since he converted to Islam while in prison, but Savage still called him Bama.

Life couldn't be better for him. He was leading by examples as a Muslim, staying true to his word and the promise he made in the pen.

There was so much violence going on in the streets. He sometimes had a killer itch, but he let Savage handle his own issues while he played the background in the mosque.

Since he was already up, he grabbed this Quran and did some studying to prepare for the speech he planned to give at his Jummah service the following day.

The previous year had been the worst year ever for Savage and his crew. He'd lost a lot of good men, and friends.

The beef with the Zoe Pound was big in the city of Miami. The two crews were at war over Sam's murder, which was at the hands of Savage as revenge for his father's murder.

Big Zoe had been murdered by an unknown killer, who also killed his wife, Jada, and her unborn seed. Jada was only a couple of weeks pregnant.

"Hey, babe, what you doing in here with the lights off?" Britt said as she walked into the kitchen with heels on and her bikini stuck in her pussy.

"Damn, baby, you gotta stop creeping up on me like that," Savage said, sitting on a stool with his Draco on the counter next to him.

"Boy, please shut up," she replied, walking over to him and sitting on his lap.

"You look nice," he said, feeling on her fat shaved pussy.

"I'm about to go hit this pool, then take some pics for the gram. I just hit one million followers yesterday," she said, touching his long dreads.

"Oh yeah? Good for you. The DM better be empty," he laughed.

"It's always empty. I be blocking them goofy niggas, boo. I'm happily married."

"I know, love. But what you doing later? You know I'm trying to get a taste of this," he said, fingering her wetness.

"Uhmmmm," she moaned, kissing his lips and trying to control her horniness.

"No, I can't, baby. Sorry, I got class at one p.m. so I'll be meeting you at the mosque. I'm sorry," she said, slapping his hand and feeling his hard dick.

"Okay. I'm sure we will finish this later," he said with a smirk, looking at her fat ass poking out with a cuff at the bottom.

"I bet," she said smiling.

"Oh yeah, Bama, well Abdulla, wants to see you. Since you converted, he ain't stopped talking about it. And I can't lie, I'm proud you a Muslim now," he said, happy his wife had recently become a Muslim.

"I did it for Allah, not you. But that nigga really changed. He really on his deen. I just hope the old Bama doesn't come out," she started laughing.

"I hope not, also," he said, reading a text.

"We all should have change in our life sometimes. That's why I became a Muslim woman. Plus, who wants to sin for life? I'm trying to go to paradise, so I submitted my soul," she stated.

"I'm happy for you, Britt. I see you growing as a woman. But I have to go, love. I am going to call you later," Savage said, getting up and kissing her.

"Okay. I am going to take my swim, then go to school. Then I'll meet you at Jummah," Britt said, walking off as her ass jiggled side to side like a wave with a bounce.

***

After Britt swam, she got dressed in a black garment and a hijab, covering her face in 98 degree heat, but she was used to it now.

Britt attended the University of Miami, and spent most of her time in school and babysitting.

She forgave savage for cheating on her a while back with Jada. When she found out, she was crushed. She had still never told him that she was the one who killed Big Zoe, Jada, and her unborn seed.

Her brother, JoJo, was traveling the world, living life, while her older brother, Mice, still held his own in the feds. She'd just paid a new appeal lawyer, who found something new under a new law that could get him back in court.

She was supposed to be on her way to class but she had other plans. She was going to study with a class mate named Asia at her apartment.

Britt parked her gray Cadillac CTS-V behind Asia's apartment complex in Coconut Grower, near the train station.

She already knew Britt was coming, so there was no need for her to call. Britt grabbed her Yves Saint Laurent bag and exited her car. The lot was empty with nobody in sight, which was weird to her.

Britt took the stairs to the fourth floor, where Asia lived.

Once at her door, she knocked once, and Asia rushed to open it. She'd been waiting on her.

"Hey, girl, come in," Asia said, holding the door. She was wearing a pair of black booty shorts and a long t-shirt that read "RIP Big Zoe 4ever I love you."

Asia was a beautiful woman. She was an ex-stripper, now a full-time college student, at the age of 25 years old.

She was Haitian and Cuban, but she looked more Spanish, with golden skin, long, thick hair, almond-shaped hazel eyes, and a sexy smile, with deep dimples.

The two met in English class. Britt saw a picture on Asia's screen saver of Big Zoe and her, which made her befriend her to find out who she was.

Turned out, she was Big Zoe's side bitch. He was tricking with her. He'd even paid for her college tuition, Benz, and crib.

"What's up with you? Grab a seat. Let me go snatch my book. This exam is driving me crazy," Asia said as she went to the back.

Britt went straight into action. She placed a silencer on the tip of the pistol she'd gotten from her spouse.

Asia was in her closet looking for her textbook.
"Got it," she said, standing up from the floor turning around. She almost shit herself

"I'm sorrrry, Asia. You a good girl, just fell in love with the wrong nigga," Britt said, pointing a gun at her, seeing how scared she was.

"Huh," Asia said as she felt warm water flowing down her legs and hitting the carpet. It was piss.

"I killed Big Zoe, if you was unable to put two and two together."

"I thought we was friends. Please. I knew you was a part of ISIS. I won't tell a soul," Asia shouted as Britt looked at her as if she was insane.

"Okay, whatever. Psst. Psst. Psst. Psst. Psst. Bullets riddled her frame as the impact made her fly into her closet as she took her last breath.

Britt walked out of the bedroom, grabbed her purse, and left with a smile. She had to kill everyone that Big Zoe loved.

***

Big Art's life had been hard, both mentally and emotionally, since Gangsta Ock's death. He was his best friend, and Art felt like it was his fault because he'd brought him to Miami.

13

When he died, he had the body shipped to D.C., where Gangsta Ock was born and raised.

The only good thing that happened for the big man was his big wedding, a couple of months ago, to his new wife, Meka.

Meka was an amazing woman. She and Britt had become best friends since she'd lost Shea to the murder.

Big Art brought a nice four bedroom house in the suburbs, surrounded by white people. He'd gotten away from the violence, trying to keep his wife safe.

The thing he loved most about Meka was that she had her own eats, businesses, and money. She didn't need nothing from him.

Everything was good in married life. Growing up, he'd learned from the old heads to keep business away from home.

"Good morning, baby," Big Art said, jugging Meka from behind while she was cooking. He was ready to eat and go to work.

"It's afternoon, nigga," she said turning around and feeling his big dick on her wide fat ass while she kissed him, shaking her head.

"Boy, stop being so nasty. I have to go to work," she said, walking around in the kitchen in her heels.

"I see you still able to talk and walk after last night," he said smiling.

"Bae, please, I had you talking like Bill Cosby. Pudding," she said laughing.

"Yeah, whatever. That's why, without that makeup, you look like Whoopi Goldberg," he said, laughing as she playfully hit him. He always made her laugh. That was why she loved his company so much.

"You got jokes. Let's see how hard you laugh when I deep-throat your whole dick again," she said, grabbing his dick.

"Girl, you better stop. I told you I'm trying to fuck," he said as she walked off, swaying her hips.

"I gotta go to work and open up," he said, talking about his restaurant called Southern Lova, which was rated four stars in customer ratings.

"Ok, text me at work, baby," Meka stated.

Big Art came up with an idea to open a restaurant with Savage last year and it was a brilliant idea because he knew the feds will be closed since Bama was home.

Big Art went to work and Meksa went to work also this was an everyday thing for the couple.

***

Opa-locka, Florida

Lil Shooter was riding around in his Audi R8 coupe. Lil Snoop was riding shotgun with a SK under the seat, listening to Fetty's song "Trap Queen."

The two had Miami and Jacksonville on lock with the drug game. They kept the murder rate high with their team of young killers, ready to kill for the fun of it.

"Damn, folk, I miss the homie, Fresh. There isn't a day I don't think about the big cuz. You know today his C-Day," Lil Shooter said, driving past some projects as kids admired his car.

"Yeah, I feel you, cuz. But are we going out to Club Liv tonight?"

"I don't know," Lil Shooter said.

"What's up with Bama? I thought he was supposed to be a cold blooded killer. This nigga running around in a garment, selling Qurans," Lil Snoop stated, shaking his head as his dreads hung to his stomach.

"You can think that nigga a lame if you want. He just on his deen. Don't let that shit fool you, cuz," Lil Shooter said, laughing because he knew how Bama got down.

"Whatever. But I just bagged this bad joint from New York the other night. Shawty Puerto Rican, you know them NY bitches be mixed with all type of shit," Lil Snoop said as they passed the Liberty City sign.

"Yoiu ain't fuck, bitch nigga."

"Fuck outta here, hoe ass nigga. I got that bitch blowing my phone up, talking about she love the way I talk," Lil Snoop said laughing.

"We gotta hit up Porky projects, then go to the trap on Lafayette St. Somebody robbed us," Lil Shooter said, shocked.

"Damn, bruh, that's crazy. I wish a nigga will rob some shit in Carol City or Overtown. I'll kill a hoe ass nigga bloodline," Lil Snoop said, being honest.

"There's been a lot of Mexicans in that area lately, and in Jacksonville, all M5-13 niggas. I hate them niggas," Lil Shooter said.

"Yeah, me too, but them fools be putting in that work, no bullshit. Them niggas vicious," Lil Snoop said.

Once they went to Porky PJ's to pick up some money, they went to Lafayette Street. There were three young niggas outside pacing in front of the yellow rundown house.

They walked into the crib, which was dirty, with empty bottles, dirty clothes, and mold all over the place. Everybody was in the back room, as always. This was a fiend's house, who they gave crack to daily so they could do as they pleased in the house.

As soon as they stepped into the room, they saw Lil X holding an AK-47 at the door. He was only fourteen, but deep in the field. He had recently been shot six times, about three months ago, and survived.

"Who the fuck is this?" Lil Shooter said when he saw a Mexican with tattoos all over his head and face tied to a chair in the middle of the empty room.

"This is one of the niggas who robbed us, big homie," Monty said, standing next to the bloody Mexican.

"It was hard trying to snatch him up last night outside of the Mexican bar across town, where all the Mexicans were. He put up a fight, until Big Gotti knocked him clean out and tossed him in the truck."

"How you know he robbed us? He is a fucking Mexican. They don't even come on this side of town," Lil Snoop said.

"Him and his home boy were selling our stamped dope. We the only ones in Miami who stamp our shit with the Pillsbury dough boy," Monty stated.

"You motherfucker," Lil Shooter said as he took his pistol out and slapped the Mexican so hard that his two front teeth flew out.

"Both of you can bounce, cuz. We got this," Lil Snoop said, escorting the young goons out of the room.

"Who sent you?" Lil Shooter asked the man, looking in his eyes and seeing his hatred for blacks.

The Mexican was silent because he knew if he was to tell them, his whole family would be killed.

Lil Snoop saw the MS-13 tattoo sign on his head, so he knew he was gang banging, just like every other Mexican in Miami. Lil Snoop grabbed a pair of vice grips he saw on the floor near a bicycle.

Without hesitation, he gripped the Mexican man's small balls and squeezed as he cried out loud. Lil Shooter covered his mouth with a dirty towel on the floor.

The man was sweating as he started talking in Spanish, which Lil Snoop understood and spoke, thanks to his mom, who was Cuban and Dominican, so she only spoke Spanish in the house with him.

Lil Snoop asked him in Spanish who sent him. The man said something, but Lil Snoop thought his mind was playing tricks on him, so he told him to repeat it.

"Asesino is back and we takin' over Miami and Jacksonville," the Mexican said with an evil grin. "We know who you all are, and we're coming Asesino is here," the man said in Spanish, spitting out blood. Lil Snoop was so shocked that he couldn't move as Lil Shooter looked at him to see what he was saying.

Bloc. Bloc. Bloc. Bloc. Bloc.

Lil Snoop shot the man five times in the head.

"What he say? Damn, why you kill him?" Lil Shooter asked.

"He said Killer is back in town," Lil Snoop said as Lil Shooter's heart stopped, feeling a new war was on the rise. But he was confused as to why Killer was rolling with Mexicans.

Chapter 2
Old Ways

Killer sat in the backyard of one of the biggest mansions in Key West with one of the most powerful men in the Cartels.

Montana was the head of a Mexican Cartel family that was violent, dangerous, rich, powerful, and controlled 47% of the drug trade in the southern states, as well as Cali.

Killer washad been hiding out in Mexico City with his boss for years, ducking the feds because he was wanted for the R.I.C.O. act. He was also hiding from Savage, because the beef was at his doorstep knocking. After his pregnant girl-friend and close friends were killed, he had to relocate until the air cleared.

Montana had known Killer for over 12 years, ever since he was a little snotty nose kid, running around trying to sell nicks of weed, and skipping school. Montana used to get his Bentley cleaned every Sunday at a carwash where Killer worked on Sundays as a kid.

He took a liking to Killer. He always saw something in him. That's why he took him under his wing.

Montana was in his mid-fifties, but he looked younger be-cause he took care of himself, with his strict diet, wall climb-ing, and running.

He had a team of killers trained to go into combat. He also was one of the main leaders of the MS-13 in the states, and their homeland in El Salvador, San Salvador.

"How's everything going?" Montana asked, sitting at his outside bar under a large tent, looking at the gray clouds.

"I can't complain. It's good to be back home." Killer started smoking a cigar, a habit he'd just recently picked up.

Killer had an army already stationed in Miami, Jackson-ville, and Atlanta. His goals were to take over turfs with his

MS-13 soldiers, who were willing to die at their leader's demands.

"Does the jungle, or ghetto, whatever you call it, like the new coke and dope we flooding the community with?" Montana asked. He wasn't a big fan of blacks, he only did business with them. Besides that, he looked down on them.

"It's great, but I believe we have a road block," Killer said, while Montana looked at him.

"I got a lot of immigrants out here working hard to regain our power in the streets, so just lay low and run our empire," Montana said.

"I'ma make sure Savage and that nigger lover Papa Goya dies at my fingertips," Killer said as Montana nodded, hating even hearing the name Pap Goya, his rival. The two had a long history of beef.

"We will run Miami again soon, believe me," Montana stated.

***

Savage was sitting in Jummah, Indian style, listening to his brother and best friend, Bama, give the Ka'bati (Islamic sermon).

There were over eighty Muslim men sitting in rows as the 35 women all sat in the back.

"A man or woman with no faith is worse than a person with AIDS on their deathbed because those who reject faith and Allah are not believers. This life is hell for the believers, and paradise for the disbelievers," Bama, A.K.A. Abdulla, started reading something on paper as he talked.

"We were all sent here to worship Allah alone," he said as people slowly nodded their heads because talking at Jummah was forbidden.

"I am ending the Ka'bah on this, Angels are recording everything we do and say so I just want my brothers and sisters to be on point and aware someone is always watching," he said before he called the Muslims to prayer.

After the prayer, everybody went their separate ways to tend to their daily activities.

"Damn, Ahkee. I must say, that was great. Nobody fell asleep on you this time," Savage said, walking into Bama's office with Britt, both dressed in garments.

"Yeah, whatever, I want to see you try to give a sermon. You'd be scared shitless. I can see you now, heart racing." Bama said, sitting behind his desk with no shoes on his thick carpet as the scent of incense could be smelled miles away.

"Nice officer," Britt said, sitting down.

"One of the sisters offered to paint it so I let her. But how's college? I heard you a bossy lady nowadays," Bama asked.

"Yeah, college okay, and you know Lil Smoke going to keep a nigga bossy," she said.

"How's the religion coming along? I know this fool is not helping you, but we have classes up here, four days a week," he said, reading something off a piece of paper.

"It's ok, just trying to get this Arabic down pack and learn more searches for my prayer," she replied.

"Ok, good. Allah loves those who are patient with their deen," Bama said as Savage was texting.

"I have to make a run, Bama. We'll see you later Malcolm X," Savage said laughing.

"Okay. Please stay outta trouble and protect your life from the Shaytan (Devil)," Bama said as they left. Abdulla pulled out a loaded Colt 45 from under his desk, which he kept for war in the name of Allah. He stared at the gun, loving the power he felt with it, before he placed it back in his drawer.

***

Savage and Britt rode home in his white and red Rolls Royce Wraith in silence, both with different thoughts on their minds.

Britt was thinking about how good it felt to kill Asia. The thought of having blood on her hands turned her own.

Savage was thinking about getting out of the game, and just raising his family because he had everything a nigga could want, millions, homes, a family business, cars, and happiness.

His guards were two cars behind him. He never went anywhere without them. As soon as he got on the highway, his phone rang. Since he was driving, he told Britt to put it on speaker on the TV monitor in the dashboard, which he'd had installed weeks ago.

"Talk," Savage said, seeing Lil Shooter's face pop up.

"Boss, we have a problem. I need to see you ASAP," Lil Shooter stated as if something was wrong.

"Okay. Get the folks together and y'all know where to meet me at," Savage said before the line disconnected.

"Is everything ok, baby?" Britt asked, listening to the whole conversation and wondering what happened.

"Everything good, baby, believe me. But what you plan to cook tonight?" he asked, changing the subject, which upset her.

Britt looked out her window, without saying a word. She hated when he tried to treat her like a housewife.

She'd been there since day one, when it was only her, Savage, Big D, and Bama, beefing with the whole city. She was more gangster than most niggas, and she wanted him to acknowledge that.

She knew whatever was going on, bodies were about to be dropping.

***

Big Art was in the back of his restaurant in his office, watching the comedians because he was bored.

It was Saturday, July 4th weekend, so it was a busy weekend. He wanted to make sure his employees were just as focused as he was.

Big Art heard a light knock at the door. He told whoever it was to come in.

"Good afternoon, sir, I just received a fax from the bank, granting the business loan for the new car dealership," Ms. Lee said while walking all the way in to give him a stack of papers she'd just received.

"Damn, this is a blessing. Thank you," he said, looking her up and own because the Salvatore Ferragamo dress she wore with heels would turn any man on. Her 36-38-38 frame was curvy with ass for days, even though it was fake.

"No problem," she said smiling, looking at his big muscles poking out of his Valentino shirt.

"Ms. Lee, I'm sure your boyfriend would hate to see you leave the house in that amazing dress. Big Art stated as she turned around, blushing.

"I'm sure he would, it if I had one. But men these days can't handle all of this," she replied, walking out, her ass bouncing with every step.

Ms. Lee was twenty-four, Korean and Black, light brown with chinky eyes, and thick. She was beautiful and often mistaken for Mary J. Blige, the famous singer. She was a bad bitch with everything going for herself.

Big Art never cheated or desired another woman while with Meka because she was everything he needed.

Chapter 3
The MS Crew

Atlanta, GA

Killer was in Club Onyx throwing money on the naked stripper, who was twerking on stage, from upstairs in his VIP section with his goons.

He was sipping Dom Perignon 1995 white gold Jeroboam from the bottle worth $201,127. He looked at his Platinum World Time watch that was worth three million dollars.

Killer had bought a mansion in the Buckhead area of Atlanta the previous week, just to stay out of Miami and focus on rebuilding his empire with his new crew.

Chulo and Flaco were Killer's capos when he was itinerant. They were all in the VIP section with thirty Mexicans surrounding them, all gangbangers.

Chulo wore a Fendi shirt and pants. He had pretty hair, hazel eyes, and was clean cut. He looked like Prince Royce, the singer from New York.

He was full blooded Mexican, just like Flaco. The two had been in Atlanta for some years now, doing it big. Chulo was a loud, graven killer, who loved to bust his gun and it gave him a rush. He ran Zones 1-3 in Atlanta. He had it on lock. For only 18 years old, he was on top of his game, thanks to Montana.

Flaco was the complete opposite of Chulo, all around the border. He was quiet about his money, a thinker, humble, and loyal to his family.

He grew up in a cartel family, so he was taught the game early, especially with Montana being his uncle.

Zone 6 was all his. Flaco had the Eastside of Atlanta on lock as well as Zone 4 and 5. Atlanta's inner city was divided into zones, but it was a big city, 85% black and 90% gay in the ghetto.

Flaco disliked clubs or public places because it brought attention, but Chulo loved Atlanta's crazy night life.

The men were at the same business with some Gangster Disciples from Bankhead, who would re-up over 100 keys from Killer every week.

Killer was in the VIP with Savage on his mind, but he was imperturbable until it was time to put his plans in motion.

Flaco tapped Killer on his shoulder to inform him that his guest was on the way upstairs.

Skip and Dedo Loca were both GD's from the west side. They used to be stuck up kids until they started moving packs. Both men were over 6'4" with shoulder frames.

The men entered the VIP section and greeted each other.

"I've been hearing it's some new prices in town for the low, cus," Dedo Loca stated, sitting down.

"As far as I'm concerned, I'm the only nigga in town with prices in the teens, besides Flaco and Chulo, and I'm sure they would never hop in my move. So anybody else is irrelevant to me," Killer said as he moved his long dreads from his eyes, showing his tear drops.

"Ight, folk, I just wanted to see if they were your people, but the money's on the truck," Skip stated, showing his diamond princess grill.

"I'm sending Flaco to give you the 105 bricks, but make sure that money right. Last time you was short. Next time, I'll take that as disrespect," Killer said as Chulo looked at both men with a wicked smile, knowing they were trying to run game.

Killer stopped talking and stared at the dancers on stage, letting them know the meeting was done. Both men left, feeling like bitches. They grew here, he flew here. If he didn't roll so deep, and with the two deadliest niggas in the city, they would've robbed him and threw him in the trunk.

Once the men left, it was time to have fun. Killer had a thot that worked in the club. Blonde Diamond was a slim young dancer with light skin, long, blonde, fake hair, and tattoos. She was from New York, but resided in Atlanta.

"Hey, Zaddy, I ain't even see you come in. why ain't you call me and spend money on me, instead of them stank pussy bitches?"

"I ain't know you was at work," he said as she came in the VIP wearing high heels and a one piece green G-String outfit, covering her nipples and pussy, which was looking like a hamburger sandwich.

"Yeah, whatever. What are we doing tonight? Hey Flaco and Chulo," she said, sitting on his lap.

Both men just nodded their heads, paying her no mind because they'd both already run a train on her last year.

She was a freak, but her head game and pussy was killing every bitch in the club, hands down.

The only thing Killer hated about her was that she was a sack chaser, but he respected her grind.

"Can I go home with you tonight? I need some of that good dick, Zaddy," She said, twerking her round, soft ass on his dick.

"Yeah. Go get dressed and hurry up," he said, drinking out the bottle as she ran out the VIP to get dressed.

Once outside, they took up half the parking lot with trucks for their goons and 3 luxury cars parked side by side.

***

Miami, FL

Savage stood in the basement of his barber shop, dressed in a Brooks Brothers suit, staring at a group of the most trusted men he'd ever met.

Even Bama was present, which said a lot. But because of the issues at hand, he figured he should have been present, even though he told Savage he wasn't coming hours ago.

Bama had his Muslim men waiting outside. He had his own small army that was about the Mosque, but also gangsters.

"I thought you weren't coming," Savage said to Bama, who wore a black garment, sporting his beard, while everybody else wore all back.

"When it's time for war amongst the believers, we all must fight side by side, brother," Bama stated coldly.

"Hamduiallah," Big Art said. He liked Bama's style, and was blessed to have another beast on the team.

"I ain't Muslim, cuz. I'm banging, but I still believe in the higher power," Lil Shooter said, since they were on the tpoic of religion.

Lil Snoop looked at all of them as if they were crazy. He already had a dislike for the Muslim man, and now he thought he was just taking up space and in the way.

"Listen, gentlemen, I just recently received word that my number 1 enemy is back in town, Killer," Savage stated with a spin.

"Ain't no fucking way," Bama said, shocked and confused because he thought Killer was dead.

"Yeah, gentlemen, he is back in Miami under the protection of the Cartel and MS-13 gang members. I don't even know how this shit happened?" Savage said, trying to figure out how a black nigga was a part of any Mexican organization.

"Damn, I been seeing alot of them niggas lately in Jacksonville and out here," Lil Snoop said, remembering the words of the Mexican he killed with Lil Shooter.

"Their leader is Montana, a very powerful man, from what my connection tells me. And the two don't see eye to eye. He controls Mexico with the drug trades but I plan to send him back to Mexico in a casket," Savage told them.

"So you telling me we are about to go to war with the Mexican Cartel and the MS-13?" Lil Snoop asked, knowing if so, there was about to be a lot of blood spilled all over Florida.

"Both, bruh. Montana runs both organizations and supplies all the head Black Hand Leaders with drugs so they're under his command from the west to the east coast," Savage stated. He'd done his research.

"They are trying to take over and somehow Killer is putting the better in the back," Bama said softly, knowing how a nigga like Killer thought.

"Facts. So from this day forward, it's war. Any Mexican gang tries to sell drugs in your neighborhood, toe tag them all," Savage stated.

"Everybody stays on point and has goons at all times," Big Art stated. "We can't lose no more good men," he said, thinking about Gangsta Ock.

"I hope we can all make it out alive. But please understand, this life isn't meant to be lived until we die in the name of Islam," Bone said with the look of death in his eyes.

Lil Snoop mumbled something under his breath. Then he leaned over to his left to Lil Shooter, who was looking at the ceiling, planning to make it up out of this war alive. "That nigga would, bruh," Lil Snoop said as Big Art overheard the comment and chuckled. He didn't trust a damn thing, but he knew Savage's judgment was 100%.

"Yeah, but he rock solid. You're going to see, bruh. Watch," Lil Shooter stated as they wrapped up their meeting.

***

Savage made it home at a good time. As soon as he walked in his mansion, Britt was sitting in the living room.

Britt was naked, sitting on the couch with a pair of Jimmy Choo shoes on, playing in her fat pussy, and moaning.

Savage's dick got hard at the sight of her thick legs spread open like an eagle. She took her finger out of her soaked pussy and pointed at him, inviting him to join.

He heard the gushy sounds of macaroni as she stuck two fingers in and out of her pussy.

"Ummm. Shit. I'm coming," she shouted as her toes curled and Savage got undressed.

"Oh, yes. Oh my god, I'm about to nut," she screamed as she busted a big nut on the leather couch.

"Damn, you happy to see me?" she asked.

"Of course," he asked.

Britt smiled and stood up to kiss him. Their warm bodies felt warmer together. He looked at her nice, perfect, firm perky titties.

Britt lightly rubbed his hard dick. Then she dropped to her knees as he stood up in the up in the middle of the floor. She slowly kissed his black dick, as if she was kissing him. She started to lick his balls while massaging his dick at the same time.

"Ummmmm," he moaned.

"You like that," she said, doing two things at once.

"Yes, baby," he said.

Britt went back to the tip of his dick and started sucking it like a lollipop, in slow motion, as if she was Pinky the porn star in her prime, before the STD's

Once she saw his body tense up, she knew she was doing the right thing. Britt started to deep-throat his dick without choking. Then she came up and dived on it again, taking it in her throat. Her eyes got watery as she started to bop faster and faster until she felt his cum dripping out.

"Shit. Yes," he moaned, while holding the armrest of sofa as she was bopping fast on his dick. She was sucking and making loud slurping noises as she went. Savage couldn't take it anymore. Her head game was so good that he wanted to cry and dance at the same time.

"I'm about to bust," he said with his eyes shut tight.

Britt continued to spit, slurp, and suck his dick with her thick lips.

As soon as he came in her mouth, she swallowed every drop of semen. She even caught the cum dripping down her chin.

"Shit."

"Baby, that was scrumptious, daddy," she said, licking his dick clean.

Savage was still horny as he picked her up from the floor and bent her over on the couch. He slowly pushed his hard dick into her tight walls, making her scoot up.

"Ugghhh," she moaned as he started to go faster, once her tight walls opened.

"Fuck me. Ugggg, fuck this pussy harder, baby," she moaned, throwing her ass back.

Savage started to go hard, as she liked it from time to time. He rammed his dick in her from behind.

"Ohhh shit, yes."

Savage slapped her ass, making it red, as her ass bounced everywhere, while he went to work, feeling her cum.

"Oh shit, I'm climaxing," she yelled.

She was in pleasure and pain as she felt the massive dick inside her.

After he nutted, he ate her out, causing her to almost pull his dreads out of his head as she climaxed again.

"Let's go upstairs. That was the warm up," he said, smiling.

"Boy, fuck no. You not going to tear my walls out. Then I have to go get a new pussy, like the bitch off Black Ink," Britt protested, out of breath.

"I'll pay for it. Now came on," he said, walking upstairs with is dick swinging.

"Oh my god," she said, walking funny because her pussy was already sore and she knew she was in for a long one tonight.

Chapter 4
Summertime Shootouts

Atlanta, GA

Powerful and his crew were a household name in Atlanta. They were heavy in the drug trade, and in raising the murder rate from Stone Mountain to Zone 3.

Powerful's family was big in Atlanta and Miami, where he was raised with his older brother, Damn, who was murdered years prior to his move from Miami to Atlanta.

At twenty-five, he was living a crazy life already. Two years ago, while living in Dade County working for Savage and Big Art, he'd caught a double homicide, and beat it at trial.

Once he came home, Savage sent home back to Atlanta to open up shop with 200 keys, and he'd never looked back. But he only dealt with a very select few, to keep the feds out of his business.

There were only a few hustlers who knew Powerful had keys. Normally, he was in his hood, shooting dice in Bankhead projects or College Park on the south side.

Powerful was leaning on his sky blue 96 Impala on 28 inch rims with all-white interior, blasting 21 Savage's album from his speakers.

Powerful was 6 feet tall with dark skin, six fat dreads hanging to the middle of his back, and a platinum grill.

Before Powerful started fucking with Savage, he and his brother, Damn, used to re-up from the Mexicans. Flaco and his people, who had the city on lock, was his former connect.

"Nah, look, find my money or move out of my city. If I gotta send my goons at you, then you know what it is," Powerful yelled into his trap phone to a fiend who owed him $25.

Powerful didn't play about his money. He'd once killed a nigga over $7.50 in a Checkers parking lot, on Glenwood Road.

A black truck was pulling up slowly on the block. Powerful noticed it, while everybody else was shooting dice on the wall, smoking, drinking, and talking shit, all unaware of their surroundings.

Powerful knew everybody's car in the hood, and he'd never seen this car, which gave him a funny feeling.

When the truck stopped and its headlights shut off, Powerful grabbed his AK-47from his backseat and yelled for everybody to duck. He knew it was a hit.

The truck was coming full speed as masked gunmen hung out of the windows, shooting.

Bloc. Bloc. Tat. Tat. Tat. BOOM. BOOM. Tat. Tat. Bloc. Bloc.

Powerful and his crew was airing the truck out, almost killing every person in the truck, except the driver, who was swerving. Two of Powerful's gunmen fell in the area where he was shooting. They'd suffered over ten bullet wounds to the upper torso.

One of the victims was Powerful's 16-year-old cousin, Baby Gangsta, who had been just chilling with his girlfriend, Tonya.

The whole hood ran outside after the shooting stopped to see four dead bodies. Three of them were teenagers who'd just been at the wrong place at the wrong time.

Powerful hopped in his Chevy and gave the empty AK to one of his soldiers as he pulled off, doing 70 because the cops were near. He could hear the sirens.

As he dipped down side blocks, trying to get in a safe zone, he thought about the driver and passengers' faces he'd seen. They were Mexicans.

He'd never had an issue with them, even when he stopped dealing with them, so this was unexpected.

The drive-by that had just gone down was the beginning of a new war. Once blood was spilled, there was no turning back.

Powerful was going to switch cars and lay low until he came up with a master plan.

***

Jacksonville, FL

Lil Snoop was in one of his main projects with thirty of his soldiers, watching the scene as money was flowing

Fiends were running in and out of all six buildings, copping crack and dope at ten o'clock at night. The buildings were booming, as if it was back in the 80's.

When he looked at what he'd built in his city, he felt proud. he was the man out here. That was thanks to his dead homies, Tree, Dirty Red, and Fresh. If it wasn't for them, and Lil Shooter and Savage, he would just be another gang banger in the streets.

Lately, Lil Snoop had a taste for Mexican food, mainly blood. He loved violence, it was better than sex to him.

As soon as he was about to go into one of the buildings to check on his soldiers, who were upstairs cooking coke, he heard someone call him.

One of his young niggas ran up to him out of breath.

"Boss, we caught two Mexicans selling dope to our fiends and they was telling them to never buy form them niggers," Lil Assassin said. He was 15 years old, but a live wire. Without words, Lil Snoop and four of his shooters hopped in a Chevy truck and headed towards Maple Ave.

When they reached the block, it was pitch black with a couple of apartments and a park across the street.

There were three Mexicans out there posted up, laughing. They were tatted up, wearing baggy clothes with black flags for their MS-13 gang.

"You gotta be kidding me," Foxy said, seeing the wannabe niggers posted up on their block.

Lil Snoop hopped out with the car still moving and a Draco in his hand.

"I know y'all wetbacks lost y'all fucking minds in my hood selling shit. Who sent you? I'ma give you a easy way out," Lil Snoop said, standing face to face with the biggest one. The Mexicans looked at him as if he was crazy, not caring about his goons or weapons.

"We MS-13 and we go anywhere we want. So since we here, this our block now. You got an issue with that, then holla at the big homie," the big musclebound Mexican said, with his breath smelling like liquor.

Lil Snoop laughed before he shot him in his face. Lil Assassin shot the other two men in their heads before they could even reach for the pistols under their 5X t-shirts. They left the dead men on the block. Fiends saw them laying there and went in all their pockets, taking money, drugs, and weapons to sell for more drugs.

***

Miami, FL

Bama was in the mosque in his quiet office, reading.

He was interrupted by Yasir, who walked in without knocking.

"Ahkee, I made the calls to all the brothers that you requested, and everybody is stationed and waiting," Yasir said.

"Okay, thank you, brother," Bama said.

"Of course, but I have a question. Something I've been wondering about," Yasir announced.

"What's up?" Bama asked, looking at the older man, who was sharp in religion and had been book smart since he was a kid.

"I will never question your judgment or feelings, but are you sure about this war with the Mexicans? We all knew what Savage is into, but do you think it's worth losing the lives of good Muslim men?" Yasir asked honestly, not wanting to sound as if he was scared, because he wasn't. He just wanted to die as a man in the name of righteous living.

"Brother, I hear your concerns, and I truly understand. I know you're knowledgeable about the den and you put your soul into your oath, but I will not allow disbelievers to kill believers while I sit and watch like shit is sweet. Savage is in a life of sin. That's for Allah to judge him. He is still a Muslim, so his blood, honor, and property is sacred to me," Bama said.

Yasir nodded his head because everything he'd just stated was in the Quran. "Just making sure, brother. As-Salaam-alaikum," Yasir said as he turned to walk out, ready to turn up.

"One more thing, always cover your brother's faults so Allah can cover yours on judgement day," Bama said, reaching for his Qu'ran.

"Inshallah," Yasir replied.

When he walked out Bama made a silent Dua with his hands, praying for a better way in life, joy, safety, and growth.

Bama went downstairs to lead the Muslims in their late night prayer. Then he planned to go home to get some rest.

***

Key West, FL

Savage was in Key West, FL at Papi Goya's mansion, ready for his meeting with his connect. His mansion looked like a castle connected to a castle, with bar gates surrounding the house on its own 21 acres.

He left his four guards outside in the truck to be on standby because Papi Goya had security guards on the roof, front yard, back yard, and walking up and down the mile long driveway.

Once he got inside, he walked past 13 security men who all nodded their heads at him in a respectful way.

Walking through the house was like walking through an amusement park.

Papi Goya always met him in the conference room, as if he lived there, but it was his place of business, where he felt comfortable.

Once he made it to the double doors, he softly knocked.

"Mr. Swagga, please come in," Goya yelled with his raspy old school voice.

Savage walked inside to see him sitting at the head of a long oak wood table on a laptop.

The office smelled good, like Cherry. The lights were dim, accentuating the Versace rug, leather Versace drapes hanging over the windows, and famous paintings on the wall.

"Glad to see you're on time."

"Being on time is good for business, and good business is what I'm about," Savage stated, sitting down.

"Correct, but we have a little problem, my friend. Something that reached my eyes about the last situation we talked about." Goya started shutting off his laptop, giving Savage his full attention.

"What's going on?" Savage asked

"And I told you before, I have a long history with Montana and he is protecting the person who killed your mom. They have been bringing drugs into the U.S. through your reign, kid. The two teamed up to take over," Papi Goya informed him.

"I see that now."

"I'm telling you a little story. Me and Montana grew up together in Mexico. We both started his Cartel family together, years ago. He got very greedy and tried to cross me in the game. He robbed me and shot me in the head, but luckily I survived it and strengthened myself. I took everything I had left and built my own cartel family, the Goya Cartel Family," he said proudly as he paced his floor with his hands behind his back.

"Damn, no wonder why you knew so much about him," Savage stated.

"I knew his moves before he moved. I'm 61 years old, he's 54 years old. I was on this earth longer, and I showed him the game."

"No doubt, bruh."

"I sent goons out to kill him before, but they never came back alive. He sent them all back in a body bag," Goya said seriously.

"I gotta finish the job," Savage said, a little worried, hoping his army was ready to go up against something so strong.

"Yeah, but he's back in Miami somewhere. Some old friends of ours tell me he is here, but the city isn't big enough for us both," Goya stated.

"The 305 ain't big enough for us three, don't forget," Savage joked.

"Word to the wise, whenever a lion gets tired of hurting, what will he do next?" Goya asked, letting that soak on his brain.

"A lion will then kill anything next to him to please his stomach," Savage said, knowing there was no difference between the jungle and the streets.

"Correct, kid. Now I have to catch a flight, but your shipment is here and will be in the same place and same time. Be safe and smart," Goya said, walking out into a hidden room.

***

Big Art was pulling out of his restaurant, heading home to chill with his wife on a playdate.

The following week, he was planning to open a new car dealership downtown with all exotic luxury cars, and of course rentals.

The Cadillac coupe stopped at a red light. he just so happened to look in his rearview to see a truck tailing him.

Big Art made a quick right, a left, another right, and then sped down the block to see the truck still tailing him.

He swiftly pulled out a P89 pistol from under his seat and hopped on the expressway, hitting 95mph, and ducking through the rush hour traffic.

Minutes later, he got off of exit 6, and the truck was nowhere in sight. He drove home pissed off, praying he would catch them niggas again. If so, it would be on and popping.

Once at home, he changed his attitude.

"Hey, baby, how was your day?" Meka asked. She was in the kitchen cooking.

"I'm ok. how was yours?" He replied.

"Just some crazy shit at the hospital. There has been a lot of dead Mexicans coming in. ICE police basically live in there. This shit crazy. They must be warring," she replied.

"That's cray, bae. But what you cooking? It smells good," he asked, changing the subject.

She finished cooking and they ate. Then they talked and fucked all night.

Chapter 5
In Traffic

Flaco wasn't a man of many words. He let his business and actions speak for themselves.

One of Flaco's main soldiers walked into his room.

"Sir, we had a little problem. Yesterday, one of our workers got hit, sir," Big DR said as he stood in front of his boss' desk.

Flaco just looked at him with a disappointed expression.

"Call a meeting with everybody as you exit my fucking office," Flaco said calmly.

Big DR did as he was told after exiting, but truth be told, Big DR hated the way Flaco talked down to him. He promised himself that if the opportunity over presented itself, he would teach him a valuable lesson.

Flaco hated to lose good men because that meant less money, more problems, and new recruits. A dead man can't make money, unless he was Tupac or Biggie, the thought to himself.

Flaco made a call to Chulo and told him about the meeting. He remembered Killer was in Miami handling something. Flaco saw a text message from a Dominican chick he'd met downtown Atlanta in the Underground, named Emily. She was Selena Gomez's twin.

Emily texted him, "Good Morning."

Flaco texted, "Can we go on a date tonight? You have been on my mind and I would love to take you out."

Emily texted back, "Yes, I would love to."

Flaco smiled at the thought of making love to Emily. That smile disappeared when he remembered he had to speak to his uncle about getting a cheaper price on the dope. The first thing

Flaco had to do was prepare for his meeting with both his soldiers and workers.

***

Britt was sitting at home listening to Darnell Jones album while preparing dinner for Savage and Lil Smoke, as she always did when the baby wasn't around.

Britt was making baked macaroni and cheese, fried chicken, wild rice, greens, cornbread, and sweet potato pie. She knew what her family liked. Britt's life had been a roller coaster for years, but since she'd become a Muslim, things had been different for her, mentally and physically.

Britt's trigger finger still itched sometimes, but she could only wonder when would be the next time she'd have the chance to scratch it. Killing Big Zoe, his soldiers, and Jada wasn't enough. It only made her hungrier and harder to control her desires. Britt filled their plates with food and waited on her loved ones to come in. She had extra time to make her Maghrib prayer, so she did, trying to clear her evil thoughts.

Lil Shooter was in the O-Town, chilling in the hood, waiting to pick up $400,000 from one of his youngins. He was shooting dice with a bunch of Miami killers with gold grills and palm tree dreads.

"Throw 10 racks, bruh. Anything less is a no go around here," PJ said to the crowd of hustlers. PJ was one of Lil Shooter's hitmen in O-Town, and well-respected in Miami for his charm and body count. Over twelve men dropped 10K down on the floor, including Lil Shooter. In no more than ten minutes, Lil Shooter had 120,000 in his pocket that he'd won. Seeing everybody's face frowned and down, Lil Shooter gave everybody their money back. He fed the hood, not took from it.

PJ's little soldier came running outside with 3 Gucci bags full of money.

"Good. About time, but I'ma have Terz and Hond bring you them bricks in less than an hour," Lil Shooter said as he hopped in his Impala on 32-inch rims.

"I'ma be throwing a party for Fresh this weekend. He was like Mike to the hood up here, even though he was a wild nigga, we love him," PJ said as Lil Shooter was pulling off into traffic.

Lil Shooter had his music so loud, listening to 2 Chainz and Lil Wayne's albums, he couldn't even hear his phone ring as he stopped at a red light. Once he looked at his phone lighting up, he saw it was Cherry Balm from the strip club KOD (King of Diamonds). After letting it ring, he received a picture text that said, "Baller Alert. I'm waiting, daddy," with a picture of a light skinned woman in thongs and braless.

Before he could even text back, the light turned green. But before he could even pull off, a black van cut him off. Another one crashed into him from behind, making his head crash into the steering wheel.

After realizing what was going on, Lil Shooter pulled out his 357 and put his car in reverse. It was useless because he was blocked in. When he saw the car surrounded by twenty Mexicans, he knew it was over.

Lil Shooter started to shoot out the window until his car was lined up with AR's, FN's, M-15's, and SK's. Luckily, he was only hit in the arm twice, but the Mexicans drug him out of the car on the bridge, while the sun was disappearing. Once he was out, they pulled off, leaving his Impala with dozens of enemy holes in it. But the mission was completed and the Mexicans were sure their boss would be pleased.

***

Flaco was sitting in a large, abandoned metal factory that he owned, while Chulo was half asleep, trying to keep his eyes open.

"El Migos, we have to be prepared for a war with the blacks because the city isn't big enough for us and the niggers," Flaco said to a round of men that were seated throughout the factory.

"Where we from, they all would have died. The Cartel controlled our country, no police or feds. But in America, they are not like us. So I hope you're ready to go to war, and to die for your race and country," Flaco said, kicking Chulo's chair and waking him up from a coke dream.

"Montana is building a stronger empire than what we have in Mexico, and we can't let no blacks or pigs stop us. So if you see anyone on your turf, gun them down. It's going to be a hot summer," Flaco said, followed by some sentences in Spanish, before ending the meeting.

Once everybody left, Flaco looked at Chulo, still nodding off like a dope-fiend.

"You, what's up with you?" Flaco asked.

"Maybe I was on lean and coke all night, and I had three hoes from the blue flame," Chulo said proudly.

Flaco hated the way Chulo cared for life and other's lives.

"You gotta straighten up. We are about to go to war with the blacks, and we can't sleep on them fools, so please," Flaco said seriously.

"Don't worry, Flaco, my men are trained for this," Chulo said.

"Yes, but mental and physical trainings are different, fool. If you are not mentally ready, you won't be physically ready," Flaco said.

Chulo laughed at him.

"Man, I'm good, vado. You should try to enjoy it," Chulo said as he got up and fixed his clothes. He walked out with his money, wondering why Flaco was on bullshit all the time. Chulo felt as if Flaco was a hater.

He pulled off in his Maybach, with two trucks full of goons behind him, ready to go clubbing.

Flaco had many thoughts on his mind because the city was about to spill a lot of blood and tears.

Chapter 6
Real Pain

Lil Shooter woke up tied to a steel, cold chair, naked in a dark room that smelled like piss and vomit. Lil Shooter felt the pain from his legs to his head. Four Mexicans had beat him for over two hours, while he was unconscious. Lil Shooter started to recap what happened, and was disappointed that he got caught slipping because he knew he was a dead man.

Lil Shooter heard footsteps and people chanting in Spanish at the doors. He started to be nervous, until the door opened wide.

Three short Mexicans, under five feet tall, walked in with AKS and Draco's, surrounding him. Lil Shooter's eyes were so swollen that he thought he saw six men, but that was his unclear, double vision. One of them started to speak in English.

"Our boss is on the way to Loco Papi, so I wish you the best of," the Mexican paused. "How you Americans say it? Oh yeah, luck," the Mexican said with a laugh.

"Glad you having fun. You taco eating motherfuckers," Lil Shooter said.

"You lucky the boss wants you alive because I'll kill your black, chicken eating ass myself," the Mexican that spoke English stated.

Seconds later, a man walked in wearing a suit and tie, with a briefcase, sporting long neat dreads, and looking like a lawyer from the ghetto.

Once the man looked Lil Shooter in his eyes, Lil Shooter almost choked on his blood.

"Good afternoon, Lil Shooter, long time no see. Glad you made it, but you were first on my Christmas list because I believe you shot me. Do you remember, on the wedding day?" Killer asked.

Killer said some words to the Mexicans, which made them all leave the room.

Lil Shooter wondered how a black man could be a boss in the cartel.

"I don't give a fuck, nigga," Lil Shooter said.

"Killer laughed as the door flew open, revealing the biggest, ugliest, blackest, ghastly nigga Lil Shooter had ever seen, in a dress with make-up and high heels.

Lil Shooter thought it was a joke until the faggot licked his crusted lips at him with a grin.

"I'm not fucking no man, so you can kill me now, bitch ass nigga," Lil Shooter yelled.

Killer laughed and pulled out a camera phone from his briefcase.

"Oh no, pimpin, that would be too easy. See, my mans Big Baton Rouge just came home from doing twenty years in the feds and he is here to fuck you, my friend," Killer said, while uncuffing one of his hands to cuff it to a metal table.

Once Lil Shooter was bent over, he tried to fight with his feet, until Killer cuffed his feet. Lil Shooter was now cuffed to a table, bent over, while Killer and Big BR broke his jaw and dislocated eight ribs, leaving him limp and in pain, causing him to spit up blood.

Big Baton Rouge grabbed Lil Shooter's ass and spread his ass cheeks while spitting in it. Then he lifted his dress up to pull out his horse dick. The big man rubbed the tip of his dick in his ass, making Lil Shooter jump forward. He then rammed his massive dick inside his ass, causing him to scream and cry tears.

Killer was recording it like it was a porn movie, getting every possible angle.

Big Baton Rouge started to hump fast. The ass was good to him. He started to get weak in the knees. Big BR busted a few nuts in his ass, while blood and shit dripped down his dick and legs.

Lil shooter passed out after the first nut he felt released in his asshole. But once the big man was almost done, he licked the blood and shit outta his ass, causing him to get horny again, until he saw Killer pull out a 50 cal.

"What are you doing? I want to keep him because he is special and we can use him," the big man said, while trying to block Lil Shooter.

Killer just laughed. Then he shot Big Baton Rouge in the forehead twice, and Lil Shooter in the body and face over eight times.

Killer texted Savage, telling him, "I'll see you soon," with the video attached to it of Lil Shooter's brutal death.

***

Savage was at home getting back rubs, preparing to make love again, round two. Savage laid Britt on her back and slid his dick inside her wet, tight pussy, while kissing her neck.

"Oh yesss, uhhhmmmm. Daddy, go harder. I want it rough," Britt moaned.

Savage started to go deep in her pussy, pounding it roughly, and lightly choking her. Britt dug her nails in his back. She couldn't take it anymore. Her muscle started to tighten up before she came back to back, while Savage continued to put his game down.

Once Savage felt Britt's juices flowing, he pulled out and sucked her clit while swallowing all of her cum, making her go crazy.

Once the two were done making love, Britt ran into the bathroom to clean herself up, while Savage noticed a text from an unknown number.

Once Savage opened the text, he was confused, until he saw the video. It made him sick to his stomach.

Britt walked out of the bathroom to hear Savage playing porn on his phone, something he never did, and the bitch was screaming and moaning crazy. Britt thought she had to step her game up.

"Baby, if you wanted a round 3, just ask. We don't need porn," Britt said as she sat next to Savage, who had a crazy, disgusted look on his face.

"Babe, what's wrong?" Britt said. Then she saw a big man raping Lil Shooter. She was shocked. She had to cover her mouth.

Savage saw Killer's face with a smile as he blew him a kiss. He tossed the phone, trying to hold back his anger and emotions, while Britt hugged him, naked.

Savage took a hot shower by himself, just letting the water drain his tears as he thought about all his loved ones who were gone forever.

"I gotta get some extra help to wipe them out. Who can I link with?" Savage said to himself as he thought of plans to destroy his enemies.

Chapter 7
Visit

A few days later, Killer informed his boss, Montanta, about the kidnapping and murder of Lil Shooter. Montana only had one thing in my mind, which was power. He would use anybody as a pawn until he was checkmate. He was a poisonous snake.

Montana sat in his fancy library with over 1 million books, reading the 48 laws power while puffing on a ten thousand dollar cigar. Montana heard a light knock and told his visitor to come in. Once he saw Flaco, he smiled because he was waiting on him.

"Nephew, have a seat. Good to see you," Montana said.

"Same here, uncle, but I need to talk to you about raising the prices on me. The blacks are looking for new connections. It's not right," Flaco said.

Montana just sat there, listening to him cry, but smiling to himself because he'd fallen for the trap.

"We also need more men in ATL because we have problems with the blacks there," Flaco said sadly.

"Seems to me like you can't control your turf or these niggas that will slave for pennies," Montana said, shaking his head.

"No, I just don't want to lose. I'm trying to win, but also keep the feds off of us," Flaco said, while Montana nodded his head.

"Okay, look, I'll drop the price to 19, only if you do me a good deed," Montana said putting his cigar in the ashtray.

Flaco knew it was serious because Montana never asked a man for a favor, and he had a team of trained killers to go handle his dirty work.

"I need you to go back home to Mexico and kill my brother, your uncle, Loso," Montana said as if it was nothing.

Flaco's eyes grew big because killing a family member was a death wish in the cartel.

"He raised me, Unc," Flaco said as he stood up to protest.

"You have 72 hours, and now you have 71," Montana said as he continued to read his book, as if Flaco was a ghost.

***

Once Lil Snoop saw the tape of Lil Shooter's death, a piece of him died with him. he felt lost and confused. Lil Snoop arrived at Bama's mosque to speak to him, but once he got inside, he saw over forty Muslim brothers sitting around, reading.

"Excuse me, but is the Imam here?" Lil Snoop said to a young brother who sat in front of him.

"Yes, he is in the back, brother," the young Muslim said in a low voice, trying not to disturb the "juice."

Lil Snoop had no clue it was Ramadan for the Muslims as he knocked on Bama's door.

"Come in," Bama said. He sat on the floor in the dark with two incents burning.

"Should I turn on the lights?" Lil Snoop asked.

"Should you interfere with a man's peace?" Bama asked in response, seated on the ground with his back toward Lil Snoop.

Once Lil Snoop sat on the floor, he noticed Bama giving him a cold stare that made him feel uneasy.

"I know I barely know you, but now that my best friend is gone, I feel as if the world is against me. I want to kill everybody," Lil Snoop said emotionally.

"I want to replace that feeling," Lil Snoop said.

Bama looked at him oddly. "The more you kill the disbelievers who shamed my faith, the better you feel," Bama said with a smile as he stood up.

Bama put two pistols under his garment and told Lil Snoop to follow him.

After tonight, he would wish he would have gone to a preacher. Both men left the mosque and hopped in an all-black hooptie.

***

Powerful had been laying low since the drive by shooting, but tonight was payback. He was in one of the two black Yukons that were carrying soldiers, dressed in all-black, with ski masks.

Powerful did a lot of homework on the Mexicans moving weight around the A, and Tum Tum was first on his list.

Tum Tum was a fat Mexican, who sold bricks for his boss, Capo.

***

Tum Tum had just come back from his re-up of a couple of keys. He was talking big money shit to his soldiers.

"Dome, I was balling and putting niggas in the dirt since I came to the A. I'ma take over soon, beleive that, cuz," Tum Tum said proudly.

Dome was a quiet type. He just wanted to get money and fuck bad mami chulos, but he couldn't wait until the day when a nigga pushed Tum Tum's cap back.

"If Capo keeps trying to raise this price on us, I'ma kill that bean eating bitch," Tum Tum continued.

"Why bite the hand that feeds us?" Dome asked.

Before Tum Tum could even curse him out, the side door flew open. There were four masked men with Draco's pointed at them.

Dome tried to run.

Lil Rabbit shot Dome over ten times, dropping him like summer flies.

Powerful stood his 6'3" frame over Tum Tum at the kitchen table, while he told his crew to kill everybody in the house and take whatever. Powerful stomped Tum Tum to the floor, while whipping him with his Draco.

"I am asking you one time, where can I find Flaco or Chulu?" Powerful asked.

"I never saw them. I'm just a worker," Tum Tum said, crying tears.

Powerful shot him with his Draco until his body laid in a blood pool. After the crew killed two soldiers hiding in the bathroom, they left $200,000 and a couple bricks richer.

Flaco arrived in his hometown of Mexico City, just about an hour away from his uncle's place, Flaco rode in the limo, wondering why Montana wanted Loso dead after Loso had taken good care of the family after his dad, Scar, died.

Loso got cut out of the family business after his wife and children were killed by his soldiers in the cartel, who worked under Montana as well. Loso did his best trying to keep Flaco away from Montana's evil ways because Loso knew firsthand how he was. Montana had even killed their only sister, years ago, because she got pregnant by one of his workers, who ended up dying with her.

Loso was a new Priest in his church, which he owned now, and Flaco was on his way to visit him.

***

Big Art was at Ms. Lee's house, eating a big dinner she'd cooked for him. He wondered why such a young, sexy, smart woman wanted to get married, but he knew she was his type of woman.

"I'm so glad you could make it," Ms. Lee said.

"I'm glad you're around. What would I do without your help?" Big Art asked, while he looked at her breasts in her dress.

"I can be your help in so many ways." Ms. Lee wore no panties as she lifted her dress up to sit on his lap.

Big Art felt her ass on his dick and he got a hard on. Ms. Lee felt his massive dick grow and she took advantage. She pulled down her dress straps and popped off her bra, showing her 34DD breasts while getting on her knees and unfastening his slacks.

Big Art was caught up in the moment, and he couldn't think straight. She was sucking him like a pro.

Ms. Lee sucked his dick, while humming on it. Then she started to deep-throat his dick, while doing tongue tricks.

Lee played with his cum as if it was noodles. Big Art moaned loudly, while busting in her mouth. She swallowed it all.

Big Art bent her over on the table, with dinner still on it. He slowly put his dick in her love box. It was so warm, wet, and tight.

"Ohhh yesss, dadddy, fuck this wet pussy. Fuck me," Ms. Lee moaned while Big Art smacked her ass, hitting it from the back.

Ms. Lee started to toss her ass back on his dick like a dancer. Big Art couldn't take it no more, so he nutted in her raw.

"Oh my god, I love your dick," Ms. Lee said as she got on her knees and sucked his dick until he got hard again. Then they went to her bedroom to make love again.

Chapter 8
Family Bonding

Bama and Lil Snoop drove around town for a couple of hours on a mission. They made it to their final destination, a restaurant named El de Gracia in downtown Miami. The restaurant, was owned by Montana. One day, Bama had seen Flaco and Chulo there with Killer, but he had no idea they were his targets. They just looked like money, and out of place with Killer.

Lil Snoop was sound asleep until Bama woke him up out of a crazy dream he was having about eating a human brain while lying in a lion's pit.

"Come on. We're here. It's about to close," Bama said as he saw a couple of Mexicans cleaning, eating, and talking.

The restaurant was in an upscale place surrounded by all Latin culture. There were at least four security guards posted in the back at all times, protecting a secret vault filled with dirty money.

Once Bama and Lil Snoop walked in, all eyes were on them, not because they were the only blacks in the room, but because they had on ski masks and carried big choppers.

"Everybody get the fuck on the floor," Bama said in a calm voice.

Once everybody hit the floor, Lil Snoop went in people's pockets as if it was a robbery. Bama gave him a crazy stare but as soon as he was about to say something, four big Mexicans busted through the back. Bama had to duck under a table to take cover, while Lil Snoop hid behind a wall, while bullets bypassed him.

Bama started to shoot at the two Mexicans that were trying to close him in. He shot one twice in the head, leaving his body next to an old lady, who was dead from the crossfire. The other

Mexican hid behind a table while he and Bama shot it out. Lil Snoop grabbed a male off the floor to use him as a shield.

Lil Snoop shot one Mexican in his chest four times, giving him time to move in with a headshot, killing him. Lil Snoop saw Bama and a Mexican shooting it out and cheered his friend on, screaming, "Kill his bitch ass," while jumping up and down.

Lil Snoop saw he wasn't getting anywhere, so he shot three bystanders with his AK, and then threw it on the floor. Lil Snoop had been a pro with flips ever since he was a kid. He'd been the best in his hood and school. Lil Snoop did five back flips, landing in front of the Mexican and killing him with his 357.

Bama had never seen a male flip like that. He was kind of impressed. Plus, he was tired of going back and forth with the dead Mexican. Bama heard a couple of victims crying hysterically. When he turned his head, he saw a family huddled in the corner. Two teenage females, a young boy, and their parents were shaking and in tears. Bama quickly killed them all.

Lil Snoop stood there, amazed to see a real Muslim put in work fearlessly.

"The only way I could've let them live is if they could've accepted the deen," Bama said seriously.

"How could they if you ain't ask?" Lil Snoop inquired, while making their exit, stepping over dead bodies.

"Well, brother, I don't speak Spanish," Bama said with a smile.

Once back in the truck, Lil Snoop knew why the man was labeled crazy and insane, but he didn't know how to make a killer feel better, Lil Snoop thought as he took a nap, holding his 357.

***

Flaco wished he could turn back and go to America instead of coming to Mexico to kill his blood uncle, whose only goal had been to protect him from harm.

Flaco called a team to post up at the church, where he was on his way, for back up.

Loso's life had been rough since he was a baby, but once his parents died and his brother killed his sister, he felt hopeless. Loso was the head of a cartel, which his family had left to him and his brothers. He'd rebuilt it from the ground up, while giving Montana and Scar big positions. Loso had killed many men to get to the top and was well respected still, to this day, after walking away. Loso knew death was around the corner, but he had no clue it was right outside.

Flaco walked into the huge church that had huge religious pictures of prophets, and empty benches. Flaco tried his best to creep up silently behind his uncle, who was reading a book in the front row.

"It's good to see you nephew, all big and grownup, but I'm sure you're not too happy to see me," Loso commented, still reading, not even looking back.

Flaco should have known better than to try to sneak up on a vet. He'd forgotten Loso was Mexico's number one hit man.

"Yes I am. I came to see how my uncle was doing. I've been busy," Flaco said, now face to face with Loso.

"I understand, but please cut to the chase. You're boring me. Why are you really here?" Loso asked while staring at him with his heartless eyes.

"Montana sent me, Unc. I'm sorry, but this is it," Flaco said while pulling out a 50 cal.

Loso smiled, "Yes, I know, but why? If I taught you anything, it was common sense and patience," Loso said.

"Let me tell you a story before I go to hell. Please have a seat. It's important," Loso said, patting the bench for Flaco to sit.

"Over twenty something years ago, your father, Montana, and I rebuilt the family cartel. I was the boss and killer, Montana was the supplier, and Scar was the muscle and enforcer. I was the oldest, so I was the brain. We started to see millions daily, and we had over a thousand soldiers, but people grew envious. One day, I overheard Scar and Montana arguing over how to control the family accounts," Loso said with the wheels in his mind turning.

"I stood outside the door, listening, and it was Montana who wanted control, power, and all the money. Then I heard him say, 'Scar, I deserve your position and life. I am shedding blood sweat and tears for this family.' He was yelling and seemed very upset. 'What about Loso? We're family,' I heard your father ask. I could hear his footsteps. He was walking towards the window. Then Montana put a gun to the back of his head and said, 'Sorry, brother, but there is no family at the top,' as he pulled the trigger twice."

Flaco sat there amazed to finally hear the real story. It all made sense now. Montana had been using him as a pawn for years.

"After he killed your aunty, I knew he was cold-hearted and a monster, so please watch yourself and protect your life" Loso said.

"I could have had you killed when you stepped foot off the plane. Why do you think he sent you and didn't come himself?" Loso asked.

"Luckily it's my time anyway, but it could have been years ago," Loso said as he did a bird call.

Over forty armed and trained killers came up from under benches, out of corners, and on top of the balcony, making Flaco confused and nervous.

"Everybody can go home to your family. Your years of hard work are over. I have sent money to each of your bank accounts for risking your lives while working for me," Loso told is army.

Once all of his men left, Loso smiled and lit a cigar as Montana always did. Flaco felt bad, but he had to keep his word.

"I got a date with the devil, so do me the honors, Loso said with a bright smile.

"Don't worry, I'll send you company," Flaco said as he shot Loso six times in his chest before leaving with a new outlook on the word family.

Chapter 9
Your Move

Big Art left his crib after his dinner date with Meka. He was driving his new BMW X1 truck to Savage's house. Big Art refused to let anybody risk his marriage, let alone his relationship with Meka.

Once Big Art arrived at Savage's mansion, he peeped how Savage had stepped his security up. his shit was looking like the white house.

Once inside, everybody greeted him as if he was the vice president. Lil Smoke was running around the decked out mansion shirtless, in his Power Ranger underwear, like a madman.

"Uncle Art, where were you, and where is my Iron Man toy you promised me?" Lil Smoke asked as he gave Big Art a hug.

"I forgot the toy, but I got something better," Big Art laughed.

Britt walked into the living room just in time. "Go put some damn clothes on, boy," Britt said.

Lil smoke took off running up the stairs like a bat out of hell.

"I'm sorry, Art, but what's good?" Britt said, sitting down on the sofa, wearing a Chanel dress, and glowing.

"Ain't shit, just running these businesses," Big Art said, looking at Britt's full curves that could be seen from the front in her red dress.

Britt's bright green eyes lit up in happiness, once she realized he was doing good.

"How's Meka? I haven't seen her in a while, not even at school. That's my girl. She's working her ass off," Britt said. "Savage is in his prayer room," Britt added, walking off to look after Lil Smoke.

Big Art walked downstairs into a dark room to see Savage on his knees movign his index finger around in a circular motion while praying.

Once he was done, he stood to his feet.

"As-Salaamu-alaikum, ahkee," Savage said.

"Wa-alaikum Salaam, brother. I just came to check on you and the fam," Big Art said as he took a seat on the carpeted floor.

"Thanks, but I'm in great hands. Have you seen the news?" Savage asked.

"Naw, I've been so busy with this new chick and work," Big Art said

Savage had no idea Big Art would cheat on his wife and was confused as to why. Meka seemed cool. Savage wanted to feel him in on the issue at hand first.

"There were two masked men, black they assumed, with long dreads that ran up in Montana's restaurant downtown and killed 13 Mexicans. The restaurant was believed to be the cartel stash house, but the killers ain't steal money. They just killed everybody, even kids and women," Savage said, in deep thought.

Big Art knew their crew was the only crew to beef with the cartel. Plus, the dreads was a give-away. Everybody in the crew had dreads. That was their trademark.

"Maybe we should cut our dreads off," Big Art said with a laugh.

Savage looked at him with a crazy expression as he sat in his recliner, thinking.

"Oh yes, so tell me about your affair," Savage said, shaking his head.

"Well it's a fling, not an affair, and she is my assistant. We've been getting pretty close lately," Big Art said as if he was ashamed.

"Women are like fragile glass and can see through shit like water, so we gotta be smart. I've made mistakes, as we know, but you only get one real marriage," Savage said.

"Britt is everything a man needs and wants, and I know you feel the same about Meka. So why destroy what you have for less?" Savage continued.

Big Art started to feel worse. He wished he'd never had this talk, but he felt it was time to leave Ms. Lee alone.

"We have a problem in Atlanta. Our crew is having problems with the cartel and gang members, so I am sending Lil Snoop and Bama out there," Savage said.

Big Art looked at him like he was crazy because the two of them together meant a lot of bodies.

"I miss Lil Shooter because he knew how to control issues and move without traces," Britt said, walking in on their conversation.

"What's wrong with them two, besides their reckless and ruthless ways?" Savage said with a chuckle.

"How is the hunt for Killer and Montana going?" Big Ant asked with a concerned look.

"It's getting good. We got leads in ATL and Palm Beach, also Tampa, so hopefully we'll have them soon," Savage said.

"As far as this Montana dude, he is like a ghost. But I'm on it," Savage said strongly.

"I'm out, bruh. Give me a call. I gotta open a car dealership on Friday, so Saturday let's go out," Big Art said.

"Okay, I'm down, ahkee. I also got a little plan I'm cooking up, so stay tuned," Savage said.

***

Killer sat in his condo in Palm Beach, wondering about his next move because he was out of them. Killer had a six men team at all times, no matter where he went. It had been hard for him to locate Savage. He felt the young boy was hiding two steps ahead of him.

Killer found Big Art's business in the yellow pages, which was a new restaurant that had recently opened. Killer had a couple of men following Big Art, but he always disappeared on his men, as if he knew it was a hit. Killer came up with an idea to send Savage a clear message. While lying in his king size bed, he turned to fox news. The headline news was 13 dead Mexicans found in a restaurant downtown. Killer knew who pulled the move, but he couldn't care less. He grabbed his AR-15 and tucked it under his pillow as he dreamed about killing Savage and his sexy bitch.

***

Powerful and a couple of his goons posted up outside of Capo's BM's crib in College Park, just south of Atlanta. Powerful hadn't had a good night's sleep since the drive by. He'd informed his boss about the issues and his boss was supposed to be sending a crew.

Powerful saw a blue Benz Truck pull up on rims. Capo hopped out without a care in world, carrying a Michael Kors bag.

Powerful laughed at how dumb and slow College Park hustlers were, but he knew the Mexicans were the connection on the south side.

Ten minutes later, Powerful and a three man crew walked in Capo's house as if they lived there. Once inside, they saw Capo and his ugly ass baby's mother sitting on a couch, cuddled up, and listening to Romeo Santo's video.

"Excuse us," Powerful said.

"What the fuck is this?" Capo said, moving, trying to get to his nine, until Lil Paul smacked him with his glove.

"Where is Flaco and Chulo?" Powerful asked.

Capo knew how Powerful ran the whole A. He'd seen him many times, but he never wanted to be on the wrong side of his guns.

"Listen, please don't hurt us. I don't know where the hell Chulo is, but I know he will be at the Live club tonight," Capo said, holding his broken jaw.

Once Powerful got the address, Capo's BM asked if they could leave, pissing him off.

"Well, thanks for everything," Powerful said as he shot both of them at point plank range, while smiling like a kid with candy.

Romell Tukes

Chapter 10
Cry Me a River

Chulo and his team were in Club Pin-Up turning up to the max, while listening to French Montana.

"Yo, Lil Mexico, we should buy one of these strip clubs," Chulo said, while throwing blue faces on stage.

Lil Mexico was focused on the light skinned stripper, who was bouncing her ass up and down on his dick as if her life depended on it.

Lil Mexico was a tatted up MS-13 gang leader, who was a known killer from El Salvador to Guatemala.

"If you want to be a boss, we already have the money, power, and respect," Lil Mexico said in Spanish so the stripper couldn't an eaves drop.

Chulo smiled because he loved when someone stroked his ego. "I'm almost ready to tell the homies," Chulo said.

A stripper walked up to Chulo's VIP as if she'd known him forever, but it had only been a one night stand two months ago.

"What you doing later, daddy? You know I get off soon. Why waste your money on stage if you can save it for our private show?" the Cuban stripper said.

"If I take you, mami, you know you have to fuck the whole crew, and they're freaky and careless," Chulo said with a chuckle.

The stripper knew about Chulo and his crew, every stripper in Pin-Ups did. The previous year, a stripper left the club with the crew and popped up dead in an alley garbage dumpster.

The stripper, Cuban Goddess, needed the money to pay bills, college tuition, and to support her 1 year old child.

"I'm down. I'm going to get my shit out the locker and I'll meet you in the front," the stripper said as she ran off.

Chulo thought about how good her pussy was last time and he couldn't wait to hit it first. Lil Mexico came back with a crew of ten, ready to roll out.

"I got a stripper coming with us, so please don't kill this one. Plus, she Cuban, not black. We don't need any unwanted attention," Chulo said.

The crew looked carelessly at him.

"Sorry about last time, it was a misunderstanding," Lil Mexico said with a smirk. Once the stripper came out from the back, the crew made their exit with smiles like pit bulls with food.

***

Powerful and his crew were waiting in the club parking lot for an hour, twenty deep.

"Aye, folk, that's them wet backs right there, coming out," Lil Romy said from the back seat, grabbing his first Draco.

Powerful was half sleep until his little cousin tapped him. When he looked out the tinted window, he saw the crew leaving the strip club with a bad ass stripper he'd seen around town before.

Powerful hit the button on his walkie-talkie as he saw Chulo walking towards the parking lot in the middle of his crew, without a care in the world.

"Let's make a movie," Powerful said into his walkie-talkie to his soldiers.

Lil Mexico saw about twenty gunmen pop up from under cars, behind cars, and out of cars with big guns.

Lil Mexico yelled, "en el piso tu," to his crew and boss, which meant to get down. Unfortunately, it was too late for the stripper. Her body was riddled with bullets as she died with her eyes wide open.

The crews were going back and forth with bullets. Chulo killed two of Powerful's men as he tried to make it to his Bentley. Then Powerful shot him in his leg, and all he could do was yell "Mierda."

Lil Tommy shot three Mexicans in the back as he snuck up behind them while letting his Draco off. A Mexican shot his friend, Joe, in his head. Lil Tommy saw Powerful creep up on the man and blow his brains out as if it was nothing. Chulo was still on the ground, while bullets flew like World War III. He had to move now or never, being the last man alive.

Chulo raised up, shooting like a mad man and killing four of Powerful's men. Lil Tommy was the first to drop.

Powerful saw his little cousin fall and went crazy. He ran towards Chulo with his guns blazing. Powerful was a high school and college track star. Once Chulo saw how fast he was coming, he knew he was trapped.

In seconds, Powerful was standing over Chulo with tears streaming down his face. Chulo was out of bullets. Powerful wasted no time in pulling the trigger, leaving him brainless.

***

Flaco had just handed in Atlanta this morning, after his long flight from Mexico. He was riding in his bullet proof Hummer, talking to his new Spanish chick he'd met a couple of weeks ago. Flaco's head security guard, Big Porky, was riding in the front with his boss, on his phone.

"I'll be sure to let him know, and I'm sorry about everything, Lana," said Big Porky before he hung up the phone with Chulo's sister. "She just informed me that Chulo was killed last night outside a club," Big Porky said sadly.

Flaco stared at his pinky ring with glossy eyes, feeling depressed. Chulo was a good guy, who was a team player. Flaco and Chulo had been a team since Ed, Edd, and Eddie, but Flaco felt bad because he'd brought Chulo with him to America.

Flaco felt tears from his eyes, but they were tears of pain and revenge.

"We're on our way to Killer's apartment in Stone Mountain," Flaco said oddly.

Big Porky knew whoever had anything to do with Chulo's murder was about to be the walking dead.

***

Meka was about to be on her lunch break and she thanked Allah because she was starving. Britt had called Meka last night for some girl talk and they both decided to go out for lunch.

Once 12pm hit, Meka was out of the hospital doors, headed to her new all red Land Rover truck. Meka's life was at its peak, not only for her career, but also her relationship with Art, her pride and joy.

Meka drove down the main streets, turning up the new Mary J. Blige album and singing the songs. Once she made it to the restaurant, she saw Britt's pink Bentley coupe parked, so she parked behind her.

Britt was sitting in the back of the restaurant as Savage had taught her a long time ago. Britt saw Meka walking towards her table and realized she'd gained a little weight since the last time she saw her, unless her work uniform made her look bigger.

"Hey, girl, how have you been?" Britt asked, standing up to give Meka a hug.

"I'm good, but you look amazing," Meka said, admiring Britt's outfit.

"Thanks, girl, it's Christian Siriano," Britt said, spinning around, showing off her dress that hugged her hips.

Before Meka even looked at the menu, Britt told her she'd already ordered them both the seafood fest.

"Art came by the other day. He and Savage looked so tired. I know they got a lot going on, but I wish they could leave that life alone. We're all in a good place," Britt said.

"Yeah, girl, because death or the feds is the only outcome," Meka said as the food arrived.

"How's college, and Lil Smoke?" Meka asked, wasting no time digging into her shrimp.

"Everything is great, girl," Britt said, staring at the way Meka crushed her food. Meka saw the way Britt was staring at her and started feeling kind of embarrassed. She felt it was time to tell her friend the news.

"Britt, I'm pregnant, and I need somebody to talk to," Meka said sounding worried.

"I had a feeling, girl. Congratulations but why aren't you smiling?" Britt asked.

"Because I haven't told Art yet, and I hardly see him," Meka said.

The girls talked for over an hour, and both left feeling better about each other, and closer.

Chapter 11
OT (Outta Town)

Bama and Lil Snoop had just boarded a flight to Atlanta, GA less than ten minutes ago. They were sitting in first class. The flight life was new to Lil Snoop, so he was a bit uncomfortable. Bama was calm because he was used to flying coast to coast to be transferred to different federal prisons.

"You good, my brother?" Bama asked Lil Snoop as he was sweating and seemed uneasy in his seat.

"Yeah, I'm good. Why? You think something is wrong with the place?" Lil Snoop asked with bubble eyes.

Bama had never been on an out of town mission, but he only had one thing on his mind, to clean the streets from people like Killer, for the sake of Allah. He felt as if kids should be able to walk the streets without being killed or seeing drug sales.

Lil Snoop's plan was different. He wanted to kill every Mexican that was a part of the Montana Cartel.

***

Savage was sitting in his fancy office with two private investigators, Beavis and Butthead, their nicknames given by the streets.

"Savage, we have a trail on some Mexican lieutenants here, in Jacksonville, and in Atlanta. They're part of the MS-13 and the enforcers for the cartel," Beavis said.

"The Killer person is like a ghost. We can't track him, or get a lead on him," Butthead said.

"We think you should go on a vacation, and by the time you come back, I promise you we will be on his ass," Beavis said.

"Okay, I'll go on a trip, because I want to. But if you two assholes don't have any news for me, then both of you ex-cops are fired. Why the fuck do I pay ex-cops to do a simple job, and there is always a problem?" Savage inquired.

"Sir, no worries. By the time you get back, we will have the cocksucker's grandma's address," Butthead said, smiling.

After both men left the office, Savage felt there was something wrong in their demeanor. But Savage looked at the stacks of photos of Mexicans on his table and shook his head. It was summer and Savage was ready to go on a trip while Lil Smoke was at camp for the summer.

Savage called his travel agent and told him to get him a fancy hotel, a first class flight, and a tour guide. Once he got off the phone, Britt walked in wearing skinny jeans and a Prada shirt, with her hair hanging past her shoulders.

"Hi, baby, how was your meeting? I saw the cops walk out mad," Britt said, sitting in his lap.

"Fuck them cracker red necks. Pack your shit, we about to go on a vacation," Savage said.

Britt was so busy staring at the photos of Mexicans, she couldn't even hear him. Her blood was boiling. Savage saw a crazy look in her eyes. She was in a daze.

"You heard me, boo?" Savage said.

"Oh, I'm sorry, boo. I was thinking about Lil Smoke," Britt said, covering her tracks.

"We are going to Jamaica, boo. Pack your things. Better, yet, you can go like this. We are going shopping," Savage said.

"Thank you so much, boo. We need this," Britt said, kissing his soft lips

"Save all that for Jamaica," Savage said as he gathered all the photos on his desk.

"Don't worry, I got a lot more wet for you," Britt said as she flicked her tongue ring.

Savage called one of his men go drop the folder off at Big Art's office.

***

Flaco had just left Killer's crib, but he was nowhere to be found. Plus, his phone was going straight to voicemail. Flaco remembered he was in Miami last week, but he figured he'd be back by now. Flaco knew Killer was sneaky. That was why he didn't trust him at all. He only rocked with him because of his uncle.

Flaco needed some female attention, but right now, only blood spill could make him feel good. Flaco drove to the Bankhead projects, cocking his gun at a red light. Bankhead projects were like no other projects on the west side of the A-Town, except Bowen Homes projects. But a known hustler named Shawt had Bowen Homes on lock.

Flaco pulled up to the raggedly housing complex to see a lot of black people outside enjoying themselves, which pissed him off. The sight of seeing niggas enjoying life while his comrade was dead didn't sit right with him.

"You want me to handle the boss?" Big Porky said.

"Yeah, when I die. But until then, fall the fuck back and watch how the real mafia do shit," Flaco said as he hopped out of the truck and walked over to the crowd of people smoking weed and drinking Hennessy.

Once the crowd of men and women saw Flaco, they knew he was out of place because he was Mexican and he had on an Armani suit. The women were wet, and ready to be everything to the handsome Mexican.

"Excuse me, do any of you know where I can find Powerful?" Flaco asked calmly, standing in the middle of a crowd.

"You a lost tourist or a cop, nigga?" The smallest one of the crew replied.

"We don't know Powerful, but the whole west is his crew, so if you have a problem then state it," the smallest one said as he got off the bench with a small crew behind him.

Flaco smiled. Then he pulled out a big gun with an extended clip hanging from it and shot the smallest one in the head, first. He continued shooting everybody surrounding him, even the women and the peolpe running through the projects. Flaco stepped over the dead bodies and left the property with a smile.

Flaco pulled out a Mexican flag and laid it on one of the victims' dead body after kicking him. Once he heard sirens, he ran to his Hummer.

***

Big Art was in his crib going over the thick caseload of photos of Mexicans that Savage had Big Lo deliver to his office earlier that day. Big Art never knew there were so many Mexicans in Miami because the majority of Hispanics were actually Cubans, Haitians, or blacks. Big Art studied all of the addresses. What caught his attention was how they'd all arrived in America mainly around the same time.

Big Art left his guest room to go check on Meka because she had been acting funny lately. She was locked in the private bathroom again.

"Meka, are you ok?" Big Art asked, leaning on the bathroom door, wondering if she was on the phone with a dude.

"I'm ok," Meka said as she flushed the toilet and opened the door.

"I must have eaten some bad or molded food," Meka said, rushing to the bedroom in her PJs.

Big Art wasn't buying it but he left it alone because he had enough stress.

"How's work, baby? I see you've been busy putting in hours. I'm proud of you," Meka said.

Big Art didn't know if it was a trick question or not. He wondered if Meka knew he was cheating.

He hated Meka working for the white man, but he respected her independence. He wished she would come manage his new car dealership.

"I'm working hard, baby. I know how you feel about me working, baby, but I have to provide for us and our child. I am an independent woman," Meka said.

Meka saw the look on Big Art's face and realized she'd slipped up.

"Baby, you pregnant? How come you ain't say shit? Yesss," Big Art said as he hugged and kissed her.

"I was scared. I ain't know if you were ready for this," Meka said, pointing at her little tummy.

"I was born ready for a family, boo. I am giving up the streets as soon as I deal with this little issue, I promise. I am giving you and my son the world," Big Art said.

"It may be a girl," Meka said, smiling, showing her pearly whites. Meka was horny, so instead of talking, she pulled her man's dick out of his slacks. She sucked and slurped his dick. After deep throating him and swallowing his cum, she got down on all fours and Big Art made love to his wife while she cried in pleasure and happiness.

Chapter 12
Jamaica

Savage was standing on his balcony, staring at the beautiful view of a beach with crystal clear water at their five-star hotel. Savage stressed about the fact that Killer and Montana were still alive. He knew he had more manpower than they did. He also felt it was time for a baby of his own. Last, but not least, he was ready to get out of the game and let Lil Snoop control it.

Savage felt bad for bringing Bama back into the game because he'd become a monster, but he knew Bama was his true friend.

Britt woke up while Savage was on the balcony. She interrupted his thoughts by rubbing on his shoulders, wearing thongs and braless, showing her perky C-cups.

"You okay, baby? You look worried. Is there anything I can do to make you feel better?" Britt asked in a sexy voice.

Savage turned to face her. He intended to tell her ",no" until he saw her light brown, hard nipples, and her phat shaved pussy poking out of the red thongs.

"I'm sure we could think of something," Savage said, walking her into the master bedroom and watching her ass jiggle. Savage loved to see his wife's body. It was a true southern blessing. With no ass shot, she had a 27-inch waist, 42-inch hips, and no stomach.

Britt sat on the edge of the bed while Savage stood in front of her, pulling off his wife beater, showing his six pack and tattoos. Britt was so wet she was sweating in her palms. She was ready to please her boo. Britt undid his Robin jeans and Gucci belt, and pulled out his manhood while rubbing his balls. Britt then sucked him like she missed him.

Britt moved her hand and started sucking the head of his dick like a lollipop, using her tongue ring.

"Damn, baby, suck daddy dick," Savage said.

"Ummhmmmm," Britt moaned, going deeper on his dick to feel it in the back of her throat. She was bobbing up and down like a pro.

Britt spit it on his dick while sucking the pre-cum from the top of his dick to let it drip down her chin. Savage came in her mouth moments later, and she swallowed everything. He got weak in the knees.

Savage laid Britt on the bed and propped her legs over his shoulders while putting the head of his dick into her wet, tight pussy. Savage served short pumps until he got all the way inside her warm pussy because it was so tight. Britt was digging her nails in his back.

"Yes, baby, fuck me. Oh my god, that's my spot, baby. Stay right there," Britt said as Savage pumped harder, almost putting his whole dick in her.

Savage did cardio and lifting 4-5 times a week, so he had stamina, but Britt's pussy was so good that a normal dude wouldn't last two minutes inside her.

Britt came three times in a row on his dick while screaming for more. Savage pulled out his dick, which was covered with thick cum. Britt got on her knees and sucked her cum off of his dick before she bent over on the bed. She buried her head in a pillow to hold her scream for what was about to come.

Savage slid his dick into her pussy slowly. Britt felt his dick in slow motion but she wanted to be fucked.

Britt threw her ass back, making her ass clap against his thighs and balls. Savage grabbed her waist and started to pound her wide ass like a beast, causing her to scream in the pillow while pulling the sheets back.

"Ohh fuckkkkk, yessss," Britt yelled, cumming at the same time as Savage.

Savage laid sideways and fucked her from the side until he came inside her. Then Britt got on top and rode him like a bike until she came and was out of breath. Britt hopped off his dick and began to suck it until he got soft and was cumless.

"Thank you, baby. I love you, and I love our sex. You make me feel loved and special," Britt said before getting under the covers to go asleep.

"Love you more, sexy, and I'm here for you," Savage said as he cuddled behind his wife and lover.

***

Killer had been up at 5am for the last couple of weeks, hunting the haunted. Killer was parked outside of Big Art's restaurant, waiting for him to show up.

Killer looked at his red Rolex and realized it was past 9am, which meant it was time to open. Killer had been watching the restaurant for a week now, and he always saw a pretty young lady open up.

Ms. Lee hated opening the restaurant because it wasn't her job, but the employee who used to open up had gone back to college last week. It was a big day for her because she was going to reveal her pregnancy to Art, hoping he would be as happy as she was. She couldn't care less about his wife. She'd forgotten to tell Art that she got pregnant easily. She'd already had nine abortions since she was eighteen. But she damn sure wasn't going down that road this time.

Lee pulled up to the restaurant at 9:35 a.m. with heavy bags under her eyes, due to a lack of sleep. She got out of the Audi truck with a coach bag, and opened the restaurant. Lee checked every register, turned on lights and ovens, and then filled the bar up with new Cîroc and Remy Martin bottles, before walking to her office in the back.

"Taco, maybe we can have a little fun with her sexy ass," Killer said to one of his gunmen, while seeing a big Yukon truck pull up blasting Scarface.

Big Art hopped out of his truck with his two guns tucked in his holsters, as always. Before Big Art walked into his restaurant, he looked around and saw a familiar truck, but he paid it no mind, not wanting to be too paranoid. Although something felt odd to him.

Big Art knew Lee was in the office because he heard her on the telephone gossiping, but when he walked in the office she hung up.

"Good morning, babe. A couple of the employees are going to be late, but I get it," she said with a sexy tone. Art wanted to address her about them stepping back, but the pussy was too good and his dick was growing just looking at her in her Prada skirt.

"Good morning, Lee. You look nice, but we are supposed to have inspections, please be on point," Art said.

"No problem, man," Ms. Lee said with attitude. Art walked out of the office to prepare for his day. He had no time for a bitch's mood swings.

Killer, Taco, and Meaty were all dressed in black, headed towards the restaurant.

The cameras were never left on overnight. They were only turned on when workers arrived. Lee had forgotten to turn them on, so Big Art's security cameras were down.

Killer and his crew tip-toed inside like mice in the projects at night. Lee was on the way to Art's office to tell him the news, and hopefully suck his dick, but once she stepped out of her office, she screamed. Taco had his gun pointed directly at her head.

"Shut the fuck up, bitch," Taco said, grabbing her and holding her like a shield. Killer was amazed at how nice and big the restaurant was. He had to admit Art had taste with his restaurant and employees.

"Pretty lady, is Big Art now pussy Art?" Killer said.

Big Art heard the scream and knew it was an issue, he cocked his pistols and left his office.

"It's no need for name calling, fuck nigga," Big Art said, pointing a gun at Killer and Taco. Meaty aimed his gun on Art, smiling.

"Glad you made it to the party. I got sick of following you around. Now where is Savage? Y'all getting on my last fucking nerve," Killer said angrily.

As soon as Big Art was about to reply, the door flew open and his youngest employee, Jason, walked in. The bullets started flying from everywhere. One hit Jason in his chest, killing him. Big Art let off three rounds in Taco's chest, killing him instantly. Killer used Meaty as a shield as he tried to grab Lee off the floor. Big Art shot Meaty in his head, while Killer grabbed Lee.

"Art help, please," Lee yelled as Killer held a gun to her head. Big Art had his gun aimed on them both.

"Shoot, nigga, I know you want to," Killer said, backing up to the wall by the kitchen exit door.

Killer pulled out a bottle with chemicals in it while he held Lee at gunpoint. He saw hot water boiling on the stove to the left of him, so he lit the towel inside the bottle and threw it at Art.

The bottle blew up, causing a big fire. Killer pushed Lee to the floor and shot her in the stomach. Then he ran off toward the back exit.

"Noooo," Ant yelled, shooting wildly towards Killer as he zig zagged.

Big Art saw he was out the door, so he ran to Lee's aid while the fire expanded.

"I'm so sorry, baby," Art said as Lee's eyes grew low.

"I'm pregnant, baby," Lee said, coughing up blood. "And I'm sorry but I…" Those were her last words before she stopped breathing.

Big Art ran out the back of the building. There was no sign of Killer, just police, fire trucks, and EMS workers.

Chapter 13
Never Sleep

Lil Snoop and Bama arrived in Atlanta, ready for action and clapping. Once outside the airport, both men wondered where their ride was at because it was too hot to be posted outside.

Powerful and his team pulled up in two BMW X5 trucks, looking for some dread-head gangsters outside the airport, but he saw only a Muslim, a teen, and some white chicks.

Bama saw the two BMW trucks full of goons looking for somebody, so Lil Snoop flagged them down. Powerful pulled up in front of the duo, praying Savage hadn't sent these two.

"Damn, we been here for an hour, bro. you Powerful?" Lil Snoop said with an attitude as he opened the truck door to get in with Bama behind him.

Powerful and his new team drove in silence to Decatur so he could get his guests comfortable and update them on the bloodbath. Once at the complex, Bama liked the neighborhood. It was a little too decent for some. After both trucks parked in the garage in the basement, Powerful hopped out with his swag on a million with his crew behind him, walking towards the elevator. Lil Snoop and Bama followed them into the elevator quietly. Powerful looked at Bama's garment and shook his head. They got off on the top floor, which was the penthouse.

"This is y'all home, so make yourself at home," Powerful said in a sour voice.

Once the men toured the apartment and put their belongings inside their rooms, the duo came back to the living room.

Powerful stood in the living room, thinking about Savage's mistake. How and why would he send him a teen and a Muslim? Was it a joke? Powerful thought.

"I'ma fill you two in on what's going on and why I called for enforcement," Powerful said with a funny look.

"That's good, but please excuse me for one minute, brother. I have to go pray," Bama said, walking towards the backroom.

Lil Snoop saw the crazy look on Powerful's face.

"He is a Muslim, but don't sleep because he will wake you up quick. Believe me, I know," Lil Snoop said.

"And how old are you? Do you even know how to shoot a gun?" Powerful said with a laugh.

***

Big Art was pissed and hurt. His bitch was dead with his unborn child. Lee was really starting to impress him. Big Art called Savage for the 30th time, but only the voicemail picked up. So Big Art drove to the mosque, which was blocks away.

Big Art walked into the mosque and greeted all the brothers while looking for Yasir because he was the Emir.

"My brother, are you okay? You look confused," Yasir said as he gave his brother Art a hug.

"No, I'm not. The dude who Savage has been looking for almost killed me and succeeded in killing my side chick and unborn child," said Art.

Yasir's face was tightening up because Art was a good Muslim, he just was involved with wrongful things, but no Muslim was perfect.

"Do you know where this person can be found?" Yasir asked calmly.

"No, but I have his workers' and soldiers' info. I'm sure they can lead us," Big Art said.

Yasir called fifteen Muslims to the back and told them it was time. Everybody speed walked to a private room an came out with vests, Dracos, AKs, SKs, hunting knives, pistols, and gloves. The Mosque was also where Muslims were trained in martial arts, and they all went to the gun range twice a week to prepare for battle. Once Yasir said Allah Akbar, everybody made their exit behind him.

***

Hours after Powerful informed the duo about the events, they both looked bored and careless.

"Where do these niggas be at?" Lil snoop asked while texting a college bitch who went to Clark Atlanta University. He'd known her for years and was hoping to fuck while he was in town.

"They are everywhere, but mainly on the south side and every strip club in the city. They are big tricks," Powerful said, referring to the Mexicans.

Bama walked outside toward the balcony, counting his fingers. Powerful walked behind him, calling his name, but he didn't move.

He couldn't figure out why Bama was so weird and quiet, but he wanted to inform him that this shit was serious and he needed him to wake up.

Powerful touched Bama on his shoulder, causing him to turn around in slow motion with a crazy look that sent chills down Powerful's spine as he quickly backed up. Luckily Lil Snoop broke the stare down.

"I say in a hour we ride on them niggas and keep it old school," Lil Snoop said, smiling.

An hour later, Powerful, Lil Snoop, and Bama arrived at Club Strokers to see four low-riders parked in the front. The club never really had security like the others, so that was a plus. Lil Snoop was ready to toss some money at some Georgia Peaches. Bama was about to be the only one in the club in a Muslim garment, but before Powerful could say anything, they were already in the club.

As soon as Lil Snoop and Powerful were walking towards the stage, they saw over 15 Mexicans staring at them, but they were just trying to throw money. As soon as Lil Snoop threw a blue face, bullets started to thunder from the bar, hitting strippers and Mexicans. Everybody was running around like chickens. Lil Snoop wasted no time, he shot for Mexicans in the VIP, who had been grilling him.

Two Mexicans were shooting back, until Bama hit them with his choppers. Lil Snoop saw a couple of Mexicans duck, walking to the back.

Powerful hadn't seen any Mexicans to shoot because shit was going down so fast. People were dropping, falling, running, and screaming. It was a massacre. Two dark Mexicans were slowly creeping up behind Powerful. As soon as Powerful turned halfway around, Bama gave the Mexicans two head shots. Powerful couldn't believe he was living like that in his garment. Bama continued shooting up the crowd, killing innocent people for being in the wrong place.

Lil Snoop caught the Mexicans at the back exit door because it was chained. He shot them all one by one while singing "Wangsta" by 50 Cent.

Back in the front, six Mexicans came running out of the bathroom, busting at Bama and Powerful.

"I take the left and you take the right," Bama said as he ran left, dropping two Mexicans like hot fries. Powerful shot two Mexicans in the chest while he ducked fired from the other two, who stood in front of the door.

Lil Snoop creeped in from the back door to see two Mexicans shooting. He shot them both in the back of the head and stepped over their bodies, as if it was too easy.

As they made their way out Bama grabbed a Mexican who looked black that was dead and cut his tongue out. Then he stabbed him in his eyes. Bama wasn't done. He reached into the Mexican's pants and cut his small penis off, saying "this will lead you into the hell fire." Powerful almost vomited on a dead stripper, while Lil Snoop laughed as he walked out the back.

"We have to go before the Atlanta PD get here, boy," Powerful said as he exited the front door with Bama behind him, walking calmly as if nothing had happened.

On the ride back, Bama and Lil Snoop were having a deep discussion about Malcom X and MLK, as if they hadn't just killed over thirty people.

Powerful wondered if they were even humans, but now he prayed to stay alive and out of the white men's system because these two niggas were death.

"What's the plan for tomorrow?" Lil Snoop asked.

"I hope nothing, but thanks for saving my life, Bama," said Powerful.

"Don't thank me, thank Allah. your day will come. I just hope you accept the deen," Bama said.

Powerful turned up the music because there was something about Bama that creeped him out.

Chapter 14
Art Work

Savage and Britt were enjoying their trip to Jamaica while wining and dining on the beach, jet skiing, and clubbing. Britt had just gotten back in from shopping and sightseeing in Kingston. Savage had just woken up to join his wife in the living room. Britt opened her laptop and checked Savage's emails to see if Lil Smoke's camp emailed him, as they did weekly.

Britt saw an email form Art, so she clicked on it to be nosey. Once she did, she realized it was written in code with numbers. Savage walked up on her to see what she was doing.

"What you doing, sexy?" Savage asked as he hugged her from behind.

"Oh, I was checking to see if the camp emailed you, but instead it was Big Art," Britt said, moving out the way.

Savage sat down to read the email. Once he broke the code down that he made up, Big Art told him a hit was made on him by Killer but he was ok. Savage emailed back in code saying in two days he'd have a meeting with the top soliers. Savage slammed the computer shut and walked into the bathroom to shower. Britt knew to leave him be at times like this.

***

Over the last couple of days, 53 Mexicans had been brutally murdered. The folder Savage had given Big Art was almost empty, thanks to the help of his fellow Muslims from the Mosque.

Big Art, Yasir, and three young Muslims rode in a van to the new Mexican bar that was a known hangout for gang bangers and prostitutes. Big Art rode around the block twice before he parked and hopped out accompanied by a big black man with dreads.

Once they reached the front door, the security felt something odd about the crew, so he stopped them.

"Excuse me, but the black bars are up the street, unless you are here for business," said the big Mexican, who was covered in prison tattoos.

The crew stood their ground as two more security guards came out.

"No, I'm here for business for Jihad," Yasir said.

The security guards all looked at each other. Then they told them to get fuck away from there.

Yasir and Big Art wasted no time. Yasir shot two of the guards in the face, while Big Art shot the other one. Then they rushed into the bar, firing shots.

The bartender pulled out a shot gun and fired shots, hitting one of the Muslims in his stomach, dropping him.

Montana sat in his business office with his security, talking to two private investigators, Beavis and Butthead.

"Well, bossman, he put a pretty big penny on you and Killer, but god forbid he finds out we work for you. Our families' lives are at risk," Butthead said.

"I think you two fuck faces should let yourself out before it's too late," Montana said in his Spanish accent.

Beavis and Butthead had been in Montana's office for over thirty minutes trying to mil him, but it wasn't working. They were trying to play both sides with Savage and Montana, only to receive more money for both of their whereabouts.

Both men left the mansion pissed the fuck off. "I told you to let me talk, dummy," Beavis said.

"I got an idea. I'll have Savage kill that fucking bean-eating bitch, but I'm charging him a mill for his whereabouts," Butthead said with a smile.

"Yeah, I hope it works. If not, we are dead men," Beavis said, pulling off in his crown vic.

The two were so deep in her thoughts that they didn't even noticed the black van that had been following them for the last couple of days.

Yasir shot seven shots into the bartender's body, dropping her instantly. Meanwhile, Big Art shot two gang bangers that were heading for the back.

The other young Muslims were back to back killing everybody in sift, females and all, clearing the whole club.

Yasir lifted the young Muslim's body off the floor and carried him by his shoulders. Big Art saw five Mexicans running from upstairs, but it was too late. The two young Muslims killed them before they made it to the bottom.

Big Art walked upstairs to see rooms with beds, but nobody in them. Once he made it to room four, he saw a Mexican with a gun pointed at him, shaking. Big Art ducked behind a wall as the Mexican fired two shots. Big Art crawled on the floor, shooting him in his knees, then his side.

As the crew left, everybody had cold stares. Once they got back into the van, Yasir said a prayer as Big Art pulled off into traffic.

***

Flaco sat in one of his condos, planning his next moves. Lately, his men were dropping like flies. His price on drugs was high but the product was weak on dope and soft. He felt like Montana played him as a pawn to kill his uncle because he didn't have the balls to do it. Killer was out of town somewhere while his men were dying out here. He needed to speak to him to see who was destroying their empire.

As soon as Flaco was about to call Killer, he heard his doorbell ring twice. Only two people knew about this pad and that was Megan, his ex, and Killer. Flaco answered his door in this Hermes robe with two pistols on his side. He peeked out the peephole to see Killer.

Once he opened the door, Killer rushed in. It seemed like he was in a rush and high on soft.

"What's good, bro? I've been looking all over for you. Shit been crazy," Flaco said as he closed the door.

"I know everything, bro," Killer said.

"I need you to inform me more about who we are at war with and why because Chulo is dead and most of your army in ATL is also, bruh. So I need to know," Flaco pleaded.

"Sit down. This is a long story that will lead up to now about Savage," Killer replied. Then he told Flaco the story.

Chapter 15
Research is a Key

Savage had just boarded a private G6 jet back to Miami with Britt. They both felt like a week wasn't enough, but they had enjoyed themselves.

"Babe, we should do this again," Britt said, leaning her head on his chest.

"Sorry it had to end so fast, but I have a couple of emergencies to attend to," Savage said, kissing her soft, big, juicy lips.

Britt wanted to ask him more, but she could tell whatever it was had him upset, so she figured she should hold off on all the questions. Savage stared out the jet window, hoping to find Killer and Montana before they found him and his loved ones. First, Savage had to pay a visit to Goya to talk business and, hopefully, murder.

Savage made it to Goya's mansion in Key West just before sundown, while security chauffeured Britt home. Savage walked past the heavily armed security and walked upstairs towards the library, as if it was his home. Goya had made it clear that Savage should not to be searched because he respected his character.

Goya was in his library, smoking a Cuban cigar.

"How was Jamaica, my friend? There are lots of pretty women and beaches out there," Goya said.

Savage was a little surprised because only his agent in Atlanta, who had booked his flight, knew where he was at.

"It was cool, but I'm just trying to win the battle and the war," Savage said, changing the subject.

Papi Goya just nodded his head in agreement. "A very wise, humble, black guy once told me it's better to battle with hearts than weapons," Goya said, standing.

"Me and my men got hearts of lions," Savage said.

"No, my friend, you don't understand how to win others," Goya said, looking in his book shelf for something.

"We need a shipment. Shit getting low," Savage said.

"Tomorrow everything will be everything, as you young people say," Goya said, blowing the dust off a book.

"Oh yes, this is called 'Defeating the Soul' by Romell Tukes. He's a very good author. This book is about key strategies to succeed in war, and life," Goya said, handing him the book.

Savage thought right now was the wrong time to be reading a fucking book in a war, but he took it anyway.

"I'm pretty sure you haven't seen the news, but there is a gang war with terrorist attacks that the news is reporting daily. Lots of Mexican gangs and cartel members, including a Cuban cartel family, have been dying, but our targets are still out there. Luckily I did some research" Goya said.

***

I found out where Montana is hiding in a nice mansion. I also found Killer's Aunty, who lives in Palm Beach," Big Art said with an attitude.

"First off, brother, As-salaam-alaikum. And I do have to take time to strengthen my body and mind in times of war," Savage said, standing up to walk towards his bar for a bottle of water.

"While me and Killer had a shootout at the restaurant and he killed Lee, the woman I was fucking, who was pregnant with my seed," Big Art said as he sat on the fur rug.

"I almost had him. Allah knows I had that bitch nigga. Then he burnt my restaurant down, but he killed my unborn," Big Art said, shedding a tear.

Savage felt his pain, so he promised it was almost over.

"We gotta take these two meatball eating bitches out ASAP. They snaked me. Then we're going to Killer's aunty's house to pay him a visit," Savage said with a smile.

"Good. I'm ready, because me and some Muslim brothers have been shaking up the town to find this bitch nigga," Big Art said.

"So you're ready now?" Savage asked with a smile.

***

"Beavis and Butthead have been partners for over six years. They're not only ex-cops and private investigators, but also gay lovers. They've been a couple for years, and even live together. Since everybody in the area uses two dirty pigs that work for you, I had a team follow them around and they said not only do they work for you, but they are against you," Goya said, blowing smoke out.

Savage knew it was something very funny about the two lately, but this was a low blow. He'd invited them into his home and the whole time they were working with the enemy. He felt dumb.

"Here is Killer's aunty's address," Goya said, passing him a piece of paper.

"What about Montana?" Savage asked.

"Don't worry about him. I am taking care of him. We have some unfinished business," Goya said with a frown.

"We should kill them both now," Savage said.

"I understand your concern, but Mexicans are like a field of weeds, if you kill one, two will appear. I know, I'm 100% Mexican, so we have to do it correctly. Remember, one who doesn't use his brain is one who doesn't understand life," Goya said.

***

Big Art arrived at Savage's house around eight p.m., something he never did. Once inside, everybody greeted him with respect, all twenty something guards.

Big Art walked past the living room to see Britt praying alone in her hijab. She looked amazing. He was proud of her. Big Art walked to the basement to see Savage sitting Indian style, reading an old book.

"So you got time to go on trips and read books?" Big Art asked.

***

Beavis and Butthead sat in their living room watching The Walking Dead, cuddled up on each other. They heard a slight knock at the door, causing them to jump up.

Butthead was wearing a pair of tight leather pants with thongs under, red bottom high heels, and make-up. He completed his look with nail polish and a red wig. Butthead hid under the covers, hoping it wasn't their nosey neighbor, who was actually his little brother, because he couldn't explain this.

Beavis opened the door shirtless, wearing a pair of silk boxers. He didn't even bother to peek out the window, he just opened the door.

As soon as the door was halfway open, Beavis felt a strong kick to his chest that landed him all the way back in the living room on the floor. Butthead tried to reach for his gun, but it was too late. Savage stood over him with a 357 gun aimed at his head, while Big Art drug Beavis and laid him next to his girl.

"Well look what we got here, Dick and Butt. I knew something was real funny about y'all. First, y'all sell me out, and then you're both gay," Savage said.

"I can explain. It's not what you think. I'll do anything for you to keep this between us," Butthead said in a feminine voice.

Savage slapped Beavis with the gun so hard he knocked his front teeth out.

"Save all the faggot shit. I need info, and me and my friend will be on our way," Savage said.

Big Art hated faggots. He wanted to kill them with his bare hands.

"We still working. Give us 48 hours," Butthead said.

"Too late. I know y'all work for Montana, so did y'all give him my info?" Savage asked.

"Hell no. We are not dumb. We just tried to use him," Butthead said.

"Good, so you got five seconds to spill it," Art said.

"Hold on, let's talk about-" was Butthead's last words before Big Art shot him three times in his forehead.

Beavis ran to hold his dead boyfriend, crying and yelling. "I can't live without you."

Savage laughed. "Don't worry, you won't."

"Huhh," Beavis said before Savage blew his brains out.

"Let's go, Ahkee. I can't believe that ugly white boy had lipstick on. I know the KKK would've hung them niggas," Art said.

"Yes, you right. Let's go to my gym," Savage said as he made his exit quietly.

Chapter 16
Secrets

Flaco was sitting in his low key apartment in College Park, rethinking the story Killer told him the other night. Flaco couldn't believe he was losing good men and family members over a turf war that the cartel had nothing to do with, until now.

Flaco sat on the edge of his bed in deep thought. He was trying to come up with a plan to kill a couple of birds with one bullet. He looked at the beautiful Spanish woman lying in his bed, sleeping naked. She still looked amazing with her curves and long, jet black hair. Flaco had picked her up last night for their first date in his new, sky blue Wraith worth $350,000. She was impressed. He'd met her a couple of weeks ago in the underground mall and gotten her number, but she'd been playing hard to get.

Emily was from the west side, so she was used to getting dudded, but she knew Flaco was different. He had class, taste, and money, so she gave him some pussy on his first date. Flaco fucked the dog shit out of her all night, until the sun came up. She was Dominican and Cuban. She'd never known Mexicans were packing until she tried to fit his massive dick down her throat, causing her to almost vomit.

Flaco heard a phone vibrating. He checked his, but it wasn't ringing. When he looked at his dresser, he saw a pink iPhone lighting up like Christmas.

Flaco wasn't nosey. Plus, she wasn't his bitch, but the pussy was so good that he wanted to wife her. He just had to do more research.

Flaco took a peek at the screen and what he saw made his blood pressure go up. When he saw Baby Daddy#3 Powerful, all he could do was plan her and his funeral.

***

Powerful had a long night, and to make shit worse, one of his babies' mother had left him to babysit while she went out to a club. Powerful had been blowing up Emily's phone all night and morning. He was pissed. He promised himself she was a dead bitch when he saw her.

To make shit even worse, Lil Snoop and Bama had people scared to walk the streets. They were killing people in broad daylight, stores, Wal-Mart, gas stations, and even outside of hospitals if they looked like a Mexican gang banger.

Powerful left his daughter at his house with his sister while Lil Snoop and Bama drove with him to get some pizza from Pizza Hut.

"ATL got the biggest slices of pizza I ever saw," Lil Snoop said proudly as they walked into the pizza store.

Bama stood in the parking lot to get some air and admire the sunny day in the A.

After ordering pizza and talking about a new shipment, Powerful received a text from Emily saying, "I fell asleep at Alice's house after the club. I'm sorry."

Powerful ignored the text, but he was heated.

Once outside, they saw Bama sweating with an evil grin, and his garment was ripped.

"Follow me, I have a joke," Bama said, walking to a red pickup truck.

Six feet away from the truck, Bama stopped.

"What do you call a pickup truck with a bunch of Mexicans it in?" Bama asked with a smile.

Neither man got the joke.

"You call it dead weight," Bama said, pointing in the back of the truck

Powerful saw a woman, a teenage girl, and a Mexican man in his forties, all stabbed to death.

Lil Snoop walked off laughing, while Powerful was a little upset because they were a harmless family.

"Have a little fun. Don't keep your panties in a bunch," Bama said as he walked towards the truck.

***

"Oh my God, yesss, uhhmmmm. Art, yess, fuck this pussy," Meka yelled loudly.

Big Art was fucking Meka from behind and he loved how wet her pussy was.

"Go faster. Fuck me harder," Meka screamed as she bit her bottom lip while fucking up the sheets.

Minutes later, Big Art came inside his pregnant wife. She rolled over smiling because she was horny.

"Damn, baby, we gotta do that more often because that dick gets gooder and gooder," Meka said.

Big Art had to prepare for a meeting, so he went to the bathroom to shower up. As he looked in the mirror, he felt like he'd lost weight due to stress.

"Baby, you know the baby will be out soon, so I'm planning the baby shower," Meka said, following him into the bathroom.

"Okay, use the credit cards, boo," Art said.

"Okay, boo, I am handling it. I love you," Meka said as he went to go lay down, not wanting to stress him any more than he already was.

Big Art told her about his restaurant being burnt down in a shootout, but he never told her about Ms. Lee or his unborn child being killed.

Powerful had just dropped Lil Snoop and Bama off at the airport. He hadn't stopped smiling since their job was done. They'd killed about every Mexican gang member in the city. The news had labeled it a gang war, with over 40 deaths in a week. The murder rate was higher than it had been in twenty years.

Atlanta PD and FBI where doing point checks and random searches on highways, streets, and shopping areas because of those two. Powerful had plans to go home, smoke a blunt, and get some pussy and head from Emily, after he whipped her ass. On his way home, he received a text from Emily.

"Sorry, daddy, but I got a surprise. Hurry, can't wait for you to nut all in my mouth and fuck me until I cry and scream," Emily's text read.

Powerful almost crashed reading the text. His dick was on the steering wheel at cruise control.

Emily and Powerful had been on and off for 8 years, but their sex was always steamy. Their relationship wasn't working becaus Emily wanted a family and Powerful wanted the streets.

Twenty minutes later, Powerful pulled up in front of his crib to see Emily's Lexus LS parked on the curb, as always. Once inside, the lights were dim and candles were lit. R. Kelly was playing on the stereo. Emily came out of the kitchen wearing nothing, except whip cream on her nipples and pussy, showing her curves and DD breast.

Powerful quickly undressed and fucked Emily on the couch and floor. He nutted in five seconds, which was why Emily hated fucking the nigga.

Emily got on her knees and began suckignhis dick causing his legs to shake because Emily head game was crazy she been sukcing dicks for eighteen years.

While Emily tried to deep throat his little dick, she heard footsteps. When she looked to her left, she saw Flaco and another man standing there watching with big guns, causing her to stop.

"Bitch, why the fuck you stop?" Powerful yelled.

"That pussy good, ain't it? Only if you two weren't a thing, I may have fucked you again," Flaco told Emily.

Powerful got caught with his pants down and his gun was across the room. he was pissed.

"What the fuck you want, and how you find me?" Powerful asked with his dick hanging on his balls.

"Thanks to Emily giving me some head and me hearing her phone ringing crazy. But I believe you know why me and Killer are here, player," Flaco said.

Powerful looked at Emily. Then he spit in her face and called her a dirty bitch.

Killer had a flight to catch, so he shot Powerful over ten times while Emily screamed.

Flaco put five shots into her face. Then he walked off, telling Killer how good she was and how he should have tried the Cuban mix breed.

Chapter 17
The Final Call

Savage was on his way to a meeting in his bulletproof Hummer with two trucks full of security following him, as if he was a superstar.

Britt laid in her bed naked, playing with her pussy in the ddark. She slid two fingers in and out of her wet pussy as it made gushy noises.

"Ohhhh, yesss, fuck me," Britt said, imagining Savage was fucking her.

Britt opened her thick legs wider to go deeper as she rubbed her soaking wet fingers on her fat clit.

Ten minutes later, Britt felt her legs shake for the third time, while creamy white cum dripped down her inner thighs. She then sucked on her fingers as if it was a dick. Once she was done, she made her way to the shower. Then she heard the phone ring.

"Hellooo," Britt said with an attitude.

"Damn, sis, is that how you answer your phone?" Mice, her brother, said.

"Boy, please. Normally I would hear, 'you got a collect call from a Federal Inmate,'" Britt said, mocking the telephone system.

"Yeah, you right, but I bought an iPhone. I'm also on FB and IG all day. My DM popping, sis," Mice said.

"Boy, you so damn crazy," Britt said as she sat down.

"How's the fam? Your husband's name is heavy behind these walls, sis. People speak good of the young wolf," Mice said.

"Yeah, we great, just came back from Jamaica. I sent you 5K and gave your appeal lawyer a bonus," Britt said.

"Thanks, sis, that's love. I spoke to JoJo and he said he will be in town on business next week. He said he loved it in Mexico. Shit, he thinks he a Mexican now," Mice said with a laugh.

"Okay, good. I miss him and you. I'ma come see you next month. You still in Pollock USP in Louisiana?" Britt asked.

"Yes, I left Big Sandy after I stabbed them two COs for disrespecting my cell," Mice said.

"But listen, I have something important to tell you, sis. I have good news and bad news. The good news is my appeal lawyer got the life sentence off my back, so I could be home soon. The bad news is I have cancer, and if I don't get out in time to treat it, then they say I'ma die here," Mice said sadly.

"Britt couldn't hold back the tears because she didn't know whether to be happy or hurt. She could lose him.

"Don't worry, brother, we can beat it," Britt said.

"Yes, I know, sis, but the doc said I got a couple of weeks tops. So hopefully I make it out," Mice said.

Britt wanted to get him out herself, but that was impossible. Mice told her a guard was doing rounds and he loved her. Then he hung up.

Britt took a shower while crying. She felt hopeless for her brother, whom she dearly loved.

Savage saw a 404 area code calling his phone. He assumed it was Powerful in ATL, until he heard a kid's voice.

"Hey, boss, this is Lil D, Powerful's little cousin, may he rest in peace. He always told me to call you when it was time," Lil D said.

"Okay, no worries. It will all be okay. Hold the A down and continue his legacy, young man. I have all your info. You're in position," Savage said before hanging up.

He knew Killer and them El Migas were behind this. Powerful was a valuable player. BMF had nothing on his crew out there.

***

Lil Snoop was coming from Jacksonville about to pass the Welcome to Miami sign while listening to Plies' new album in his all-white Lamborghini Huracan LP 580-2, worth 200K.

Lil Snoop stopped at a red light, realizing it was almost time for the meeting. He hated to be late, so he pulled off. But before he made it past the crosswalk, four vans came from each corner, blocking him in the middle of the street.

Lil Snoop pulled down his window and shot his Draco towards the vans, which did no damage because they were bulletproof.

Five Mexicans hopped out of each van masked up with AK's. They turned his Lambo into Swiss cheese. Lil Snoop shot four of them, but their gun power was too much.

Lil Snoop was hit at least nine different places. He heard sirens pull up and shots transpired with the police.

Lil Snoop was barely alive, but he was able to toss his Draco on the ground next to a dead Mexican as tires burnt out on a wild police chase.

The ambulance pulled up seconds later to see Lil Snoop laying in his own blood, barely alive. They threw him on a stretcher and did 80 mph to the closest hospital, which was four minutes away.

***

Savage pulled up to the meeting to see six black trucks parked outside the warehouse and black brothers with beards patrolling the area with walkie-talkies.

Savage walked towards the back of the warehouse to a private room. When he walked in, he saw Bama and Big Art sitting there patiently.

"As-salaam-alaikum," Big Art said.

"Wa-alaikum-salam," Savage replied as he took a seat at the head of the small table.

"I'm sure Lil Snoop is on his way," Bama said.

"Yes, we'll give him a couple of minutes on the late rule," Savage said.

"You look tired. You ok, ahkee?" Bama asked Big Art.

"Well, Meka is pregnant, and I have been drained," Big Art said.

"That's a blessing. I'll be honored to be the Godfather. Thanks," Savage said.

"I hope you're ready to raise a Muslim child," Bama said with a serious expression.

"Today, children are full of racism, hate, and evil," Bama said with a disgusted look.

"I'm sure he'll be a great dad," Savage said.

"I've been seeing this woman, and it's getting serious. She may be the one," Bama said.

Both men looked at him oddly because he was always in the Mosque. They figured he just jerked off, instead of getting some pussy.

"That's good. You need it," Big Art said with a laugh.

"Well let's get started. Killer and Flaco have to be eliminated ASAP. They fucking up our family and money. They just murdered Powerful, so I'ma let his little cousin have the A. I already did my research, he's official. Papi Goya is going to take care of Montana, and if not, we will," Savage said.

Savage was about to finish until he heard a knock at the door.

Yasir walked in with a sad look.

"Excuse me, but Lil Snoop's grandmother is on the phone, crying, and asking to speak to you," Yasir said to Savage.

"It's going to be ok. I'm on my way," Savage said as he hung the phone up, and then slammed his fist on the table.

Big Art saw Meka blowing up his phone, so he answered. "Not now, baby," Big Art said.

"Baby, listen, I just saw Lil Snoop with bullets holes all in his body. Are you ok?" Meka asked hysterically.

"Fuckkkk. Yeah, I'll call you later," Art said angrily.

They all looked at each other, knowing what time it was, even Bama.

"Art, you handle the shipment and I'ma go check on Lil Snoop. There may be police and agents there, so I'ma go," Savage said.

Everybody left with their personal security. As they all pulled off, it looked like the president was in Miami, but actually it was known killers, ready to kill.

Chapter 18
Bad Visit

Savage and his six man security team walked into the ER section of the hospital. The crew looked like the men in black.

"Excuse me, Miss, but I'm looking for Shawn Wilson, who arrived thirty minutes ago in critical condition," Savage said to the black, young nurse, who looked like she'd prefer to be in a club.

"Damn, nigga, don't you see I'm on the phone?" the clerk shot back, rolling her eyes and snapping her neck.

"Listen, little bitch, if you don't answer my question, I'll turn this bitch up, with you going first," Savage said, disconnecting her phone call.

Tiffany was a regular twenty-two year old trying to make it. She looked at Savage and his men and realized it wasn't time to play Ms. Rude.

"Ten people just asked the same question in less than twenty minutes. Visiting hours are over, so most of his friends are in the waiting room, sirrr," Tiffany said calmly.

"Thank you, beautiful," Savage said, making her blush with a mean expression.

Once inside the waiting room, Savage saw there were at least twenty-something females in there, talking amongst themselves, with no males in the room. Lil Snoop's grandmother was the first to see Savage and acknowledge him.

"I'm glad he's okay, and I assure you I will take care of it," said Savage.

"I'm sure you will, but it's better to win a battle with hearts instead of weapons," the old lady said as she walked away.

Savage knew her words sounded familiar. Then it hit him, *Goya used the same phrase last week*, he thought, so he knew it had some true meaning.

The doctor came out with a smile, but as soon as he was about to open his mouth, bitches got retched.

"My boo ok?" a young yellow female with short hair said loudly, causing everybody to look at her.

"Bitch, who boo? Me and Shawn been on and off for years."

"Both of y'all bitches trippin'. I never heard of y'all. I'm his baby's mother, one and only. y'all just side pieces, better yet crumbs, dirty crumbs," a pretty brown female said.

As soon as the brown skinned chick turned around, the dark skinned Haitian punched her in her head, while the light skinned female threw a chair at both of them. Then, out of nowhere, the whole room was going crazy. Females were throwing fists, pulling wigs off, and spraying each other with mace.

Security grabbed Lil Snoop's grandmother to get her away from the mayhem, while Savage and the doctor rushed to Lil Snoop's room. The hospital security ran past them to defuse the riot.

"Sir, do you know visiting hours have been over?" the doc asked with a frown before he entered Lil Snoop's room.

Savage pulled out 8K and passed it to him. Then he walked in as the doctor moved out the way and closed the door behind him.

Lil Snoop was in the hospital bed watching "Fresh Prince," trying his best not to laugh too hard because of the gunshot wounds.

"For a nigga who got hit up, you look happy," Savage said as he sat down by the window, peeking outside.

"They caught me lacking, even though a couple of them are dead. The police just left. They said if they find out I had anything to do with the shooting, I'm done," Lil Snoop informed Savage.

"We live and learn," Savage said.

"Yeah, man, them fools blocked me in four ways. They say my car got hit 96 times, and I got hit nine. I feel like 50 cent gg-unitttt," Lil Snoop said.

"The D's told me the FBI is on all of us," Lil Snoop said.

"That's nothing new, but I know what the real reason is for that agent," Savage said. "Don't worry about them bitches. You need to worry about them girls out there trying to kill each other," Savage added.

"Damn, I know my gmom ain't call them. Fuck, I'ma dead man. I'ma just stay in here," Lil Snoop said, half-jokingly.

"Get some rest, I'll sending a team to cover you," Savage said as he left, giggling at his young wolf, knowing how crazy he was.

***

Killer hoped the hit he sent ended Lil Snoop's career after he received the info that Lil Snoop was gunned down with over 100 rounds.

Killer rode in the backseat of his Maybach while five trucks filled with goons accompanied him to Goya's mansion, only four blocks away. Killer was sure that this would be his first and last visit with the Don.

Goya sat in his recliner, reading a book called "Prisoner to Society" by Romell Tukes, and wondering why blacks and Latinos had it the hardest in society.

Goya saw his beautiful young wife walking into his office wearing a Givenchy Couture robe, looking similar to Selena in her prime.

"You hungry, papi? I made your favorite," Valerie said in a strong Cuban accent.

"No, mami, but put on some sexy clothes. I got a good feeling about tonight," Goya said while looking at his cameras to see a Maybach and several trucks pulling up to his estate.

Valerie got wet at the idea of killing. She loved sex, but killing was a forever cum. she had a body to die for and a heart to match. She put on an all-black lingerie set with two holsters on her sexy legs and two on her hips as she grabbed an AR-15 and a lollipop to suck on.

Goya saw his gate fly open as trucks pulled up with masked men hopping out. Luckily he had a 24-hour watch team because as soon as he hit his red button, shots were being fired everywhere.

"They want to fuck with the real Don? Me will show them," Goya's security team was dropping like flies by Mexicans and Valerie's aimless shooting. Goya saw 2 Mexicans running up the stairs, but then two head shots a piece had them rolling back down. Valerie was on top of the balcony, shooting every target she saw. Shit, she even shot three of her own for being in the way. But truth be told, she disliked the way they looked at her as if she wasn't loyal to her husband.

Killer walked into the mansion, stepping over bodies of both teams with a smile, as if bullets weren't flying past him.

"I came to play, Goya," Killer said in Spanish as he shot two guards to the left of him.

Killee saw a wave of bullets come his way as he ran behind a wall. He saw a female shooting at him while Goya shot it out with his men.

"I am getting him, boo," Valerie said before bullets ripped through her torso, killing her instantly as she dropped to her knees, and then landed on her face.

Goya saw his wife fall and felt tears start flowing. He started to shoot like a wild man, running downstairs towards Killer and his men.

Killer and his men were all ducking for cover when Goya came flying down the stairs. Seconds later, the shooting stopped because all of Goya's men were dead. Killer couldn't see where Goya went. It was a fake out.

"Spilt up and find him," Killer yelled to his seven man crew that was left out of 25 men.

Goya felt pain in his left leg as he ran inside his daughter's room, which was soundproof and camouflaged into the dining room wall, so she could have privacy. She was twenty four years old and beautiful, so Goya still treated her like a baby in the house. Her curfew was at 1 a.m.

As soon as Goya got four feet into his daughter's room about to turn the corner, he heard her TV moaning loudly, as if a porn movie was on. But he also realized he was shot.

"Ohhh yesss, oh my goddd. I'm cumming again. Ohhh shit, fuck me harder, papi," Tampothia, his daughter, screamed to Tom, who was a thirty-nine year old security guard for Goya. He was fucking her from behind, grabbing her small waist. "Oh no, daddy, it's not what you think," Tampothia said, once she saw Goya. Then she wrapped the stained sheets around her B cup breasts.

"It's okay, but we got company," Goya said with a smile.

Before Tom said a word, Goya blew his brains out on her pillow.

Tampothia didn't even cry or move. Tom was just a piece of dick until her man got back from DR. *Better him than me*, she thought.

"Papi, I'm sorry I disrespected you," Tampothia said.

"Don't call me that," Goya said as he blew her brains out next to her lovers'.

At least she wasn't getting gang banged, Goya said to himself as he ran to her closet to grab a 5K because he heard movement outside. He forgot he left the door cracked by mistake.

Goya heard footsteps running inside and he started spraying rounds hitting three Mexicans off top. The five men, including Killer, bum rushed the room, busting in and causing Goya to take cover on the side of the bed. Goya shot his 5K at two Mexicans that tried to jump over the bed, but then his 5K jammed. Killer heard his gun jam and knew it was a green light. Goya tried to crawl to the bathroom to get his AK, but it was too late.

"What you gonna do, what you gonna do when they come for you, bad boy, bad boy," Killer said, standing over Goya.

"I am killing you in hell, bitch," Goya said.

"Well I am killing you now, bitch," Killer said as he shot Goya over thirty times. Then he saw two of his men behind him smiling, and he killed them both before smiling and wiping the sweat off his forehead. It was serious work, killing almost forty something people in less than ten minutes.

Chapter 19
Good R Mad

Savage woke up, prayed, and made his way to his own little personal gym in his basement to exercise, which he did Mon-Fri. After an hour and some change, he made his way upstairs to take a shower because he was soaked in sweat.

After a forty minute shower, he got dressed in his all blue Sondro suit and walked into the kitchen to see Britt cooking eggs, turkey bacon, hash browns, and pancakes.

"Damn, sexy, I ain't even know you was up cooking daddy a meal," Savage said as he sat down.

"As-salaam-alaikum, and, nigga, this for me. I'm starving," Britt said in a joking manner.

"Lil Smoke, I'll be back in a few days," Britt said.

"Okay," Savage said as he went to go watch TV to see what was on the news.

"Good morning, Florida. I'm Dailen Ellingwood with the headline news reporting live from Key West," the reporter said.

Savage got comfortable on his Marchesa furniture, wondering what the fuck could have gone on in Key West. *That's the richest area in Florida*, he thought.

"Police say a well-known drug lord that ran his own cartel was murdered last night with over sixty others. Police also identify most of the shooters as Mexican gang bangers, but police still have no clue why the drug lord was gunned down. His name has not been released yet, due to security reasons. Behind me is the 45 million dollar mansion, the location of the masacre. If you have any information, please contact the FBI as soon as possible. This is Dailen Ellingwood reporting live from Key West. Back to you, Ms. Larson," the reporter said.

Savage was so stuck on the TV that he hadn't heard one word Britt said to him in the last three minutes. He was in deep thought and had to come up with a new plan, before he was next.

A couple of hours later, Britt walked into a regular Chinese buffet to meet Meka, as they had planned to hang out. Meka always chose food places because she was always driving and left her bill for Britt. Meka arrived wearing a sundress, walking as if she was 9 months pregnant, but far from it.

"Damn, you glowing girl. Maybe I need to get knocked up," Britt said.

"Oh no, bitch. Doing this shit will have you emotionally fucked up," Meka said as she sat down.

"What's going on?" Britt asked, sounding concerned, but knowing Meka could be a drama queen.

"Girl, I don't know. You know since that restaurant burnt down, Art's been acting real funny and weird, like he loved it more than me," Meka said.

Britt wished she could tell her what she overheard him and Savage talking about. How he was fucking is assistant and how he lost her and their baby in the restaurant incident, but she couldn't go against the G-Code. And if Savage found out she was eaves dropping, it would make her look as if she didn't trust him, and they'd been through enough already, she thought.

"Damn, girl, maybe you are overthinking shit. You should be preparing for the baby shower," Britt said, trying to change the topic. "I got most of the food catered from Hala Food World and Seafood Fun," she continued. "I also sent invitations to all the names and addresses you gave me. And Savage and I paid for the place to be rented for the whole day," Britt said proudly.

"Thank you so much, girl. I got the designer ready to hook it up," Meka said.

"No problem. But have you been thinking about Islam for women? It's beautiful. Look at me," Britt asked, smiling and pointing at her purple garment that symbolized her religion and way of life.

"I know you see Isis and shit, but every Muslim is not a part of that. Real Muslims hate that shit. That's not Islam, girl, that's pure evil and hate," Britt said.

"I am seeing Art pray and read his Quran, but I don't want to play with Allah. And Allah gave me these curves for a reason, to show them off," Meka ssid.

"Allah gave you a body for your husband, not for the world to lust for you. That's why we wear garments. Just do it when you're ready," Britt said as they went to fill their plates to eat.

***

It was a big day for Art. He sat in his doctor's office, awaiting the results from his STD test. Lately, he had been feeling real weak, achy, and dry, and he had lost over 25 pounds. he thought stress played a big role in this. Plus, the new baby and his street beef added to his stress. Not to mention, his wife was a pain in the ass.

Doctor Hick walked back into her office with a warm smile, as always, to see Art sweating with the AC on. He was financially good with no kids. Dr. Hick sat down at her desk and opened her folder.

"Good news, you have no STDs," Dr. Hick said with a fake smile.

"Yes, that's great, doctor. It had to be the stress. Thanks for your time," Art said as he stood up to leave the office.

"Uhmmmm, not so fast," the doctor said. Big Art was about to step one foot out her door, and then he paused.

"The bad news is your HIV test is positive, sir," Dr. Hick said with a sad voice. He went from Art to sir in one second.

Art felt as if a ton of bricks slammed him in his head because his legs almost went out. he sat down as tears rolled down his face.

Doctor Hick always had a little crush on the sexy, big man, so she kind of felt sad for him, even though she told patients they had HIV at least twice a day at her job.

***

Britt, Meka, and the designer, Quentasia, were setting up the baby shower before the guests arrived in less than thirty minutes.

Britt was helping the catering people set up, and Quentasia was putting colorful banners up, while Meka was in the corner blowing up Big Art's phone as she kept going straight to voicemails.

Meka ain't seen Art in almost two days. That was so unlike him. And his phone was off, so she was worried.

"Come on, girl. Stress later. People are arriving," Britt said.

"I still can't reach Art," Meka said sadly.

"Okay, don't worry yourself. I'm sure he is good. I'ma call Savage. Just enjoy the baby shower. Don't put no stress on my godchild," Britt said, making her smile for the first time that day.

A couple of hours and 300 gifts later, Meka was enjoying herself with her friends and family from out of town.

Britt walked outside to call Savage, and his phone went to voicemail. That was new to her, so she prayed he was okay.

Britt was going to tell Meka that Art was okay anyway, so she could stop putting stress on herself and her baby.

Britt walked back inside to see people dancing to the song "Peaches and Cream" by 112, which the DJ was blasting. Britt never saw a pregnant chick dance like Meka. She looked like she was about to twerk or drop it. Britt joined the party and enjoyed herself as she and Meka ate three plates of food each.

Chapter 20
Marriage with a Killer

Flaco hated Miami, the people, and everything it had to offer. Flaco had a meeting with his uncle Montana in twenty minutes and he refused to be late to this special meeting, so he told his driver to hurry.

Flaco rode in the back of his Bentley with many thoughts on his mind, from Chulo and Savage, to Loso. He felt like his life was closing, and he knew with the gang war going on, the Feds were on his ass. Falco loved his people, but a black person trying to control his brown pride didn't sit well with Flaco at all.

Once at Montana's a mansion, Flaco let himself inside to see many guards posted. Everybody knew Flaco. They would never disrespect Montana by searching family members. The guards told him his uncle was at the pool.

Flaco walked out back to see Montana, meditating on the edge of the pool, getting a tan on his pale skin.

"What's up, Unc? I see you enjoying the weather," Flaco said, walking up to his uncle.

"Yeah, just getting a tan, nephew. Good to see you, but you look bad. I hope you not sniffing that shit, nephew. I taught you better," Montana said, looking his nephew up and down.

"Nah, uncle, I just been busy," Flaco said.

"Yeah? I watched the news and it looks like Killer is the only one that's been busy," Montana said, getting up from the edge of the pool.

"How is the war? I hear the people like it," Montana said, referring to the black people.

Flaco wanted to say something slick back, but chose not to.

"Yeah, they lose and rake in all the money," Flaco said.

"Goya was murdered," Montana said.

"Good, no more competition," Flaco said.

"Yeah, but I wish I could've did it. That nigger lover tried to fuck up my empire," Montana said in Spanish. "Never trust blacks. They can be snakes," Montana said as he turned to walk towards his robe, which was on the ground.

"Yeah, but it's the same for your own kind," Flaco said, pulling a pistol with a silencer on it.

Montana heard the deep venom in his voice, so he turned around to see a gun in his face.

"Do you know the cartel families won't stop hunting you until you're dead, if you pull that trigger? If you don't, you're still dead," Montana said.

"Shut the fuck up, coward. You killed my parents and aunty," Flaco said with tears.

"You killed your uncle. And don't listen to Loso. He is a devil, nephew," Montana said.

"Yeah, well you two can take that up in hell," Flaco said as he shot Montana in his head three times before pushing his body in the pool. Flaco walked back inside the house to see security eating lunch, knowing their boss liked to talk in private.

"Aye, Big Lopez, uncle said he taking a swim so leave him be," Flaco said before walking out.

"Okay, youngin," Big Lopez said, while eating rice, beans and beef.

Big Lopez took a bite of his food, and then it hit him. He'd known Montana for over twenty years and he couldn't swim. He just sat at the edge of the pools.

Big Lopez rushed up from the table with nine guards following him outside to see a pool full of blood.

***

Bama was in his mosque, preparing to get married to a beautiful woman named Khadija, who was from Africa. She was twenty-two year old Muslim with light skin, grey and greenish eyes, and long curly hair. She was educated, and very smart. Her parents were from West Africa with mix cultures. Her father was a drug lord, who had raised her and her brother in the jungle. They were trained to hunt, kill, and survive. Her father was wealthy. He owned several business and homes. He was also the mayor, but he sent Khadija to America to get a better education because she was smart. She'd attended Florida State. Her brother stayed in Africa and became a hitman. She had been a hit woman when in Africa, but in the states, she was a pretty college girl.

Her parents had arrived in America days ago, since their daughter informed them about her marriage.

Once Bama met her parents, he was pleased and they were pleased with him marrying their Muslim daughter. Today was the day of the ceremony for their wedding and the Mosque was packed. Everybody was happy for the couple.

An hour later, everybody ate and talked about the new lovers. Khadija's mom was the only white Muslim woman there. She had beautiful skin and hair. Everyone admired her beauty as she left with her husband, on their way back to Africa.

While Britt talked to Khadija and other women, Savage and Bama went into the office to talk.

"Ahkee, I'm glad I got out the dirt because I thought you were a Porn Hub duck," Savage said as he took a seat. "Oh, Goya was found dead and I believe Killer did it. It was his type of scene. Now I need a new connection. I'm pissed," Savage added, taking a deep breath.

"I believe I can help you, just give me a couple of days," Bama said, rubbing his chin.

"Okay. I am hunting Killer and Flaco, but we have no strong leads. Killer's aunty is a no-show, but I believe they are around," Savage said.

Bama was so busy reading the paper, he didn't hear shit Savage was saying. "Wow," Bama said.

"Yes, I said something," said Savage.

"No. I mean read this," Bama said, tossing a newspaper on his lap.

Savage unfolded the paper to see the headline "Drug Lord Murdered in a Pool."

When Savage saw Montana's name, he knew it was a Killer or Flaco, trying to start up more of a war with every cartel family.

Both men looked at each other with no words, knowing what time it was.

Chapter 21
African Ties

Big Art checked his Breguet watch while sitting in the driver's seat of his BMW X1 outside of his car dealership. He was looking in his rearview mirror, wondering why Lee would do this to him and his family, she had to know she had it. Art got HIV/STD tests done twice a year even though he never cheated on Meka except this fatal mistake. Big Art felt like his life was at an end as he popped some medicate before exiting his car.

"Good morning, boss," Adam, his employee, said.

"Morning," Big Art said.

"I see you trimming down, boss," Adam said with a smile.

"What? Stop watching me, you little faggot, before I fire your ass," Big Art said as he slammed his office door behind him.

"He must be in a bad mood," Laura said on a low voice to another new employee.

Big Art was mad. Not only were people realizing he was losing weight, but his mind also.

Big Art saw he had a couple of missed calls from Savage and Bama, but he was too ashamed to go around them, so he'd missed the wedding.

Big Art walked into his private bathroom to pray to Allah, hoping to also cure his sickness.

Bama got off the phone with his new wife, Khadija, who was at a shooting range in Tampa, FL. Khadija informed her husband that her father would be back in town in a couple of days on business.

Bama figured that would be the perfect time to discuss business with him for Savage and his empire. Bama ran the idea by Khadija and she said she would help and set up a meeting with them plus they can't get to know each other better.

Savage was in Bama's office with Yasir, talking about life, family, and the future.

Good news, my wife said she is going to set up a meeting for us, but I fear the life you are living will have dead end," Bama said.

"I know I'm living wrong this way. When I kill Flaco and Killer, I'll give the game up," Savage said. "I am a millionaire. I own businesses and homes, and have a beautiful family," Savage added.

"You're blessed, Ahkee, and we're going to ride for you. We're family," Yasir said.

"Oh yeah, I forgot, Britt talked to Mice and he won his appeal because they took off all his time. But he is dying of cancer. Britt is fucked up behind that, but hopeful he makes it home so we can fight it," Savage said.

Bama shook his head and minded a quick Duwa for the brother, Mice.

Savage had to go check on some real estate and his barbershop/salon, so he stood up, fixed his Bule tailor-made suit, and made his exit. As soon as Savage closed the door behind him, Khadija was standing right in front of him with a crazy look on her face.

"Damn, you scared me. As-Salaam-Alaikum," Savage said, wondering how she got there so quickly from the gun range.

Khadija didn't even respond. She just looked at him with her bright grey eyes. Savage knew most foreign women were taught not to acknowledge males unless they were family.

***

Days Later…

Savage pulled up to a water deck in South Beach, looking for a place to park his Lamborghini Aventador Roadster that he'd just bought from Art's dealership.

Savage saw wealthy white people entering Yachi's ice grilling him as he hopped out his car in his Louis Vuitton suit, awaiting his friend.

Savage checked his watch to see he had a couple of minutes left before his meeting as he leaned on his car, waiting for Bama because he'd left him on the highway in a race.

Seconds later, Bama pulled up in a blue and white McLauren 12C Spider with two Tahoe trucks and a couple of cars behind him. Bama parked behind Savage and hopped out in his all-white garment and kufi.

"When did you get this? You're doing better than me?" Savage said.

"I like nice things sometimes. But my books and oil company is raking in millions. You can get with it when you 100% clean," Bama said as he walked towards the deck, and the security posted up in the lot.

Umer was Khadija's father. He hated dealing with Americans because he felt that they weren't true, honorable, or trustworthy. However, Umer had a liking for Bama.

Umer saw Bama and his friend approaching the huge Yacht named Esmeralda. Once they made it upstairs to the deck of the yacht, Umer was awaiting them.

"As-Salaam-Alaikum," Umer said with a smile.

"Wa alaikum salaam," Savage and Bama replied.

"This is nice. Damn," Bama said as he made it inside and saw two upper decks with walnut wall paneling on a 253ft vessel.

"This is one of the six yachts I own, but I own a yacht company, as well. Three of my yachts are your wife's now," Umer said.

Savage had to admit the man had taste. After the grand tour, the men sat down.

"First, I want to start by thanking you good men for being on time because if a person can waste time, they will waste mines.

"No problem, but I'ma cut to the point. I need a new connection. I lost my last one, and now I'm back to square one," Savage said. "I cop 500 bricks of dope and coke every two weeks, and that's just for Miami. I may need 300 more keys for ATL and my new location in N.C.," Savage said.

"No problem. And I assume you did business with Goya. He was a very wise man," Umer said, surprising Savage.

"I have to let you know how I operate. If anything goes wrong, you two will come up missing without a drop of DNA left anywhere. You will also put your families at risk. You're my son-in-law, but when it comes to business, that means nothing. I'm a man of honor," Umer said while pointing at his heart.

"I heard about your wars with the Zoe Pound and Bloods, and now the Mexicans. I don't pay much attention to that. Most of my business is done in foreign countries. But I do love fun," Umer said.

"No worries. We have that under control," Savage said.

"Okay, but do you know a new cartel boss by the name of Nuev Vida?" asked Umer.

"No, never heard of him."

"Well he put 100 million on your head. That's one pretty penny. At least I know you got influence," Umer said jokingly.

"You know he came to my daughter, personally, to pay for your demise, but she declined because of her husband. And may I say she is the best in Africa and North America," Umer said.

Bama listened closely. Khadija told him she was trained, but he didn't know it was this serious, and she'd never told him about Nuev Vida

"Here, go to the pickup and drop off address. Please be on time because I'm hardly in America, but my men will always be there. I look forward to your business and our friendship, Savage," said Umer smiling.

Once they left the yacht, Savage and Bama both couldn't believe how easy that was.

"Never trust a man that smiles every second," Bama said as they walked towards the parking lot.

Savage saw dead bodies on the ground, all Muslims. Bama looked around and saw nobody in sight, except dead Muslims. They hadn't heard any gunshots and his men all had their guns on them. That was a horrible way to die.

"Yo, Bama, look," Savage yelled as he picked up a note from the ground.

The note read, "F.N.K," which meant Flaco and Killer.

"We're gonna get them, don't worry. We gotta get outta here," Savage said as they ran to their cars and pulled out of the parking lot.

Chapter 22
Shahadah

Lil Snoop walked out of the hospital bright and early, after being released. He saw two blue Impalas with glossy paint and 26-inch rims full of goons waiting on him, as if he was Jay-Z. He was just glad Miami Vice Squad wasn't waiting for him because they'd been harassing him about the murders.

Lil Snoop's body was in so much pain as he slid into the passenger seat of his homie's car.

"Damn, boy. Homie, you need help?" Tiger asked.

"Naw, I'm good. But take me to the Mosque. I gotta appointment," Lil Snoop said as the cars pulled off. The driver was taking his boss where he pleased.

While lying in the hospital after that near fatal incident, he realized he needed Allah in his life. He felt it in his heart. Fuck the money, women, and drama, he needed Allah.

He was sick of seeing his grandmother stress and beg him to leave the streets alone. Lil Snoop had been a good kid in school. He went to college with hoop dreams. But he had a kid to support at seventeen and school wasn't cutting it, so he turned to the streets.

Lil Snoop was in deep thought as they pulled up to the mosque.

"Wait out here, homie. I'll be back in a second, folk," Lil Snoop said as he climbed out of the Impala in an arm cast and leg cast.

Once in the Mosque, Lil Snoop saw brothers reading, learning prayers, learning Arabic, and some just in deep thought.

"Excuse me, is the Imam here?" Lil Snoop asked a young Muslim brother who looked at to be around 15 years old.

"He is in his office," the young boy said firmly.

Lil Snoop walked back toward the office as he saw a couple of stares because of his casts and limp. They'd all seen the young man on the news anyway.

"Lil Snoop saw a lot of beautiful Muslim women in the back, talking and giggling softly.

Lil Snoop knocked on Bama's office door.

"Come in," Bama said.

As he opened the door, he saw the most beautiful woman he'd ever seen. She was light skinned with grey eyes, and looked very exotic and young. The woman had an evil look in her eyes as she stormed out of Bama's office.

"Good to see you. Please close my door," Bama said.

"I'm sure Allah decided it wasn't my time. but who the hell was that chick? I never saw nothing like that before," Lil Snoop said, sitting down.

"Thank you. She's my wife," Bama said.

"Oh shit. I'm sorry, bro. Wow. She must've felt sad for you," Lil Snoop said.

"You got a good sense of humor for a nigga looking like a mummy. now what do you want?" Bama said.

"Truth be told, I'm ready to take my Shahada and submit to Allah. I've killed, sold drugs and women, just to have a good life. But this life isn't the one I should be living. I want to move forward, and I'm ready to repent for my wrongdoings," Lil Snoop said with a tear.

Bama nodded his head.

"It won't be easy, just strive. We lose a lot of good brothers to gain more brothers in the deen. Did you research the deen?" Bama asked.

"For years," Lil Snoop said.

"Okay, let's go take your Shahada. We need three or more witnesses, but know the negativity is behind you. This is a new start," Bama said. Then he made Lil Snoop raise his right hand and read some chapters out of the Quran in front of others.

***

Hours later...

Lil Snoop reached Jacksonville, feeling like a new man. He was about to go to the projects to let his soldiers know he was home. But first he wanted to spend some time with his grandma.

After his men dropped him off, Lil Snoop rushed into his house, hoping to see his grandmom in the living room watching the news as she always did. Once he saw the news on TV but not her, he walked to her bedroom to surprise her. But as he was walking down the hall, he smelled an odor that was too familiar to him. When he opened the bedroom door, he dropped to his knees as he saw his grandmother's legs and arms chopped off, lying next to each other with a piece of paper that said, "FNK" with a smiley face. Lil Snoop vomited on the floor as tears poured down his face.

***

Khadija was sitting in her tub with bubbles, relaxing her smooth shiny skin and thinking about her husband. Khadija was upset at her father for telling Bama her business. Even though she was taught honesty, he was just too honest. The hit didn't matter to her at all. she was focused on her marriage. Khadija had killed so many people that she'd lost count years ago. It was a fun hobby to her and her brother. Many people are fooled by her grey eyes, thick curves, long hair, and pretty face, but that was all an innocent disguise.

Bama told her she disappointed him, and how could he trust a person who hid shit from him. She got pissed because she felt she was doing right by not taking Nuva Vida's offer. She barely knew Savage. But once she found out they were brothers, she was glad she rejected the offer because she loved Bama dearly.

Khadija sat wondering what she could do to please her husband and make him trust her again. She heard keys, so she got out of the tub with her perky C-cup breasts, long wet hair, and her neatly trimmed fat pussy exposed as she grabbed her towel and Mac 11.

Bama sat on his bed, pulling off his garment and revealing his chiseled body, which would make any woman go crazy. Bama felt sorry for those brothers he'd taken out to the yacht the other day. If it wasn't for him, they'd be alive. The crazy shit was that it wasn't even on the news because they were black Muslims. But if they were terrorist or white, then it would've been different.

As he got into deep thought, he saw Khadija walk into the room with a sad look on her face and her towel wrapped around her perfect body, carrying her Mac 11.

Bama loved to see her outside of her clothes because she always gave him a hard on with her perky breasts, wide hips, flat stomach, long hair, and mesmerizing eyes. Plus, her pussy was so tight that his tongue had a problem getting in and out.

"Baby, I'm so sorry for not telling you. Please don't be mad at me," Khadija said as she sat on his lap with her body dripping.

"Okay. Next time tell me because my life could have been at risk," Bama said, which caused her to get angry on the in-side hearing anything could happen to him.

Khadija dropped a tear and Bama kissed her and wiped it as she undid her towel. Her pussy was soaking wet. Bama began to suck on her hard nipples while she grabbed his head, moaning. He laid her down and took off his clothes. Once he was naked, he laid his 2 pistols on his dresser as he crawled between her legs, kissing her thick, soft thighs.

Khadija opened her legs like an eagle while Bama sucked on her clit, making her cum in seconds. Bama got on top of her and slowly put his dick in her warm, tight pussy. Once she was open, he started tearing her pussy up. She grabbing his waist and biting down on his shoulder as she screamed.

"Yesss. Fuck me," Khadija yelled.

After both of them nutted twice, Khadija got on top and rode his dick like a cowgirl on a bull. She arched her back and tightened her pussy walls. She felt herself cum three times. She'd never climaxed before and she loved it. Once Bama came, she hopped off.

"Baby, can I suck your dick and swallow your cum? I want to give you what you give me. I know I'm your wife and you don't think a wife should do it, but please," she said.

"Ok, baby," Bama said, still not wanting her to do it out of respect. Khadija sucked his dick so good he fell asleep horny and hoping for more head from her. She had the type of pussy and head a nigga would die and kill for.

Chapter 23
Sorry Ms. Jackson

Over the last couple of days, Killer and Flaco had been on a massive hunt for Savage and his crew.

Flaco come up with the idea to kill all those Muslim men at the water deck. Killer was against it because he just wanted Savage, but Flaco wanted to send a message to let them know they were easy targets.

Every time they followed Savage, he ended up losing them. They were starting to wonder if he knew. The two sat in a condo in North Miami with a beautiful white female, trying to come up with a plan F.

"Chill, pressure busts pipes. Everything is falling into place. Patience," Killer said, while getting his dreads twisted by the female, who was a random chick that he loved to fuck, named Megan.

"I don't have patience. All your men are dead," Flaco said sternly.

"We both lost, but we will get ours," Killer said.

"I am handling mines," Flaco said as he grabbed his Gucci book bag and car key, walking out.

"Damn, baby, you must've pissed him off," the blonde head female said, twisting his dreads.

"Bitch, did I ask you? Matter of fact, get on your knees and suck my dick. And you better not gag," Killer said as he smoked a blunt of Kush.

"Okay, daddy," Megan said proudly.

She loved black dudes because they had big dicks and they talked to her dirty and gangsta. that made her wet. She got on her knees and started bobbing on his dick, while playing with his balls.

Killer knew he had to get Savage ASAP before the feds got on to him. He was still on the run, but he would be carried by six before being judged by 12.

***

Ms. Jackson had just picked up Lil Smoke from his summer camp in Orlando, FL.

"How was camp, baby?" Ms. Jackson asked, driving the Range Rover.

"It was fun and I made friends," Lil Smoke said from the backseat.

"Can we get some candy, nanny? Please," Lil Smoke asked.

"Okay but first I have to drop these papers off at the Mosque for your brother," she said.

Once at the Mosque, Ms. Jackson double parked and took Lil Smoke upstairs with her as they ran in and out. She was totally unaware of the Ford Taurus that was watching.

Flaco sat behind the wheel of a stolen blue Taurus watching the Mosque closely. He'd been sitting there for over an hour, ready to go back to the condo, until he saw a pretty old woman with a crazy nice body hopping out of a new Range Rover with a young kid that looked just like Savage.

Flaco figured it was his son and the woman was the sexy woman that Killer always said was his wife. Flaco had never heard about him having a son, but he was going to make him wish he never had one. Flaco deep in thought when he saw the two of them come out and pull off in the Range.

They arrived at a Piggly Wiggly supermarket around 2 p.m. to see church people running in and out. Ms. Jackson got a lot of stares, which made the preacher look twice.

Ms. Jackson was used to the attention. She bought Lil Smoke some toys and candy. Lil Smoke loved to push the cart in the stores so she let him push it all around the store.

While Ms. Jackson was in the store, Flaco was outside in a fisherman hat under her Range Rover, putting a bomb under her truck. After he was done, he walked towards the store as if he was a shopper.

On their way outside, Lil Smoke almost ran over an old white lady with his cart. Ms .Jackson saw a handsome Spanish man smile at her. She thought if she was twenty years younger, she would give him some of her good pussy.

Once at the truck, Ms. Jackson opened her driver door and the backdoor.

"Nanny, can I put the cart back, please?" Lil Smoke requested.

Ms. Jackson looked to see if there were any cars coming, and it was dear.

"Okay, baby, hurry up," Ms. Jackson said as she hopped in the Range. As soon as Lil Smoke made it to the cart area by himself, Ms. Jackson put the key in the ignition.

Boom!

Big R, Big Lo, and Ray was told to follow Ms. Jackson to Orlando and back home, just to make sure she was safe. They were unaware of the Ford Taurus and the man in the fisherman hat that put the bomb under her truck because they were so busy on their iPhones playing games. When the men heard the loud boom, they saw the Range Rover was blown into pieces. Then they all ran towards the truck. Big R saw Lil Smoke on the ground crying and bleeding from the impact. "Call the fucking ambulance," Big Lo yelled.

***

Two weeks later…

The funeral that was held for Ms. Jackson was at the same place Savage had his mother's funeral. Lil Smoke was out of the hospital, but was on the bed rest. Britt and a heavy security team were at home with him, while Savage attended the funeral with Bama.

After the funeral, Big Art and Meka came to show their respect and to check on Savage.

"Sorry about what happened. Lil Smoke okay?" Art asked, sincerely concerned.

"Yeah, he's good, on bedrest. But I see y'all almost ready," Savage said, pointing at Meka's stomach.

"Y'all should come by the Mosque. The doors are open, and you trimming down nice, ahkee," Bama said, causing everybody to look at him and angrily.

Big Art's phone rang. It was his doctor.

"Excuse me," Big Art said, as he walked off.

Chapter 24
A Devil Smile

Killer was on his way to see his aunty in Palm Beach to give her some money, as he always did when he was in Florida. When Flaco told him he blew up Savage's baby's mother's truck. Killer was confused because he never knew Savage had a son or a bm. The news never reported a dead child anyway, but Killer thought it was best to lay low after that dumb shit.

Before Killer went to Palm Beach, he wanted to get some of his men in Jacksonville to help him because word was out that Lil Snoop wasn't dead. Killer wanted to see for himself.

Killer drove past one of Lil Snoop's projects to see him chilling on a bench, drinking Cîroc with a gang of dudes, shooting dice.

Killer drove in an all-black Impala SS to fool people, which he did. Even Lil Snoop saw his car but paid him no mind. Killer drove to Court St., where some Mexican gang bangers hustled and held their turf down, but they all worked for Flaco and Killer.

Killer saw at least ten Mexicans standing around with black flags, posted up. Once they saw Killer get out of the car, everybody tensed up. They knew he was the boss.

Killer told them to strap up, it was time. But they barely understood English. However, when he told them in Spanish, they all lifted their shirts to show her pistol. Then they hopped in different cars, following him.

Just as night was falling, the crew was turned up. They were drunk and smoking, with loud music playing, and women all around them.

Lil Snoop loved his hood and goons, but it was time to get out of the jungle, he thought as he sat on a bench by himself, thinking about all his loved ones. Since his grandmother's murder, he felt as if life was worthless. But his new religion stopped him form killing himself or others.

"Let's go to Club Live tonight. Plies, Poser Tray, and Train supposed to be there," Lil B said to one of his young workers.

"Naw, I'm good. I gotta go holla at the boss in Miami later," Lil Snoop said, taking a huge sip from his Cîroc bottle.

Before Lil B could say another word to motivate him to come, shots rang out from everywhere. Lil B caught four shots to the chest, while Lil Snoop ducked, busting back. They were being ambushed in the dark, which made it harder to aim correctly. But Lil Snoop shot two of them at point blank range.

A lot of his men were dropping as he looked for a way out. Then his soldiers started to come out of the buildings, shooting wildly.

Lil Snoop let his crew go back and forth as he ran into one of his buildings to reload. But as soon as he made it in the lobby, Killer was there with a 5K standing over two bodies, smiling.

"Never come up empty at a gunfight," Killer said, seeing Lil Snoop's gun was empty.

"You took everything I loved away. Do what you know, but you will get yours," Lil Snoop said, smiling.

"Yeah, but you're not going to be the one to do it," Killer said before shooting his 5K.

"Bok. Bok. Bok. Bok. Bok. Bok."

Killer hit Lil Snoop with all headshots, making sure he was a dead nigga this time. Killer ran out the back towards the back street to escape, leaving all of his men dead.

***

Savage sat in his prayer room, wondering how life could go from good to bad so fast. Britt knocked on the door, taking him out of his zone.

"I'm just coming to check on you baby," Britt said as she sat down Indian style next to him.

"I think we should have a child of our own soon," Britt said.

"Yeah, ok, but you saw what could've happened to my little brother. We are not ready yet, and god forbid something happens to me or my men, I want Brother Yasir and his wife to help you raise him. He made an oath to do so," Savage said.

"Baby, don't talk like that. If you go, then I go. I love you," Britt said as she stood up to leave.

Savage planned to move and get out of the game after he killed his enemy that was still lurking and working. Savage came up with an idea. But first, he wanted to make his night prayer because he was going to need it.

After he prayed, he went upstairs to get some rest. As he walked into his bedroom, he saw Britt knocked out, wearing a bra and panties set that perfectly cupped her phat ass, and two pistols on the dresser. Savage loved her gangster way. He would kill the world for her safety. Her soft green eyes spoke of love and loyalty.

***

Big Art had been so stressed lately that he'd forgotten he had a wife and baby on the way. Big Art was watching the news, thinking about his next move in life because the drug money and violence was more stressful than the HIV.

Art knew if he told Meka he had HIV she would leave him, so he had to come up with a plan. he could give it to her then act like she gave it to him, he thought. He knew Meka had been really horny lately, so he could let her suck his dick, or he would suck her pussy for hours, and then act tired or as if he had business to attend to.

He tried to use a condom the other day, saying it was good for the baby, but she went crazy, saying he was fucking other women, and he was burning. It took everything for him not to slap the shit out of her, but him eating her pussy for 3 hours made her happy.

Meka came in the door with shopping bags and a smile.

"Do you need help, baby?" Art asked.

Meka acted like she didn't hear him and put her peaches, pineapple, and fruit cups in the refrigerator. Then she went to the bathroom, as if he wasn't even there. He just sat there, looking at the door.

Art turned his attention back to the news to see that twenty-five men were killed in a gang shootout in Jacksonville. They showed photos of Mexicans, black teens, and then they showed the leader's face. "Shawn Wilson, aka Lil Snoop, a known murderer and drug dealer, who was under investigation for eight murders by the FBI," the report said.

Big Art's heart stopped and he sent Savage an emergency text saying, "Doggy Dog went to eat."

Big Art went in his room and went to sleep, feeling sad for the young kids who'd lost their lives because of a grown men's war.

Chapter 25
Nicole

Savage woke up to a text from Big Art, telling him Lil Snoop was dead. It hurt him to see his friend and Muslim brother lose his life for their crew, but that was real loyalty. Savage stared at his 62-inch TV screen, thinking of all his dead homies, Fresh, Dirty, Lil Shooter, Powerful, Gangsta Ock, and now Lil Snoop.

He wished he could run away and put all this behind him, but he'd never run a day in his life, and he wasn't going to start now. Savage got himself together, put on his garment and left his mansion, knowing Britt and Lil Smoke were asleep and security was tight.

"Yo, TJ, I'll be back in a few hours. I don't need security," Savage said to his head security guard as he hopped in his all black 600 Benz.

"Ok, boss," the 6'9" guard said.

Savage pulled up to Art's crib, texting him, "it's time. I'm outside," while hoping for a successful mission. Big Art hopped in the Benz dressed in all-black, with a champion hoodie.

Nicole wants Killer's aunty, but she had been taking care of Killer since he was a kid, while she was also young. When her sister died of a drug overdose, she was the one person who could take care of her young nephew. Their parents had died three months after he was born.

Nicole was almost forty years old, but she'd worked since she was twenty years old. People confused her for Megan Good, the actress, daily.

She'd recently retired from stripping. Seven years ago, she was the baddest bitch in Palm Beach. She did it to take care of Killer and fund her Diva ways. Once Killer moved to Miami and became a drug lord, he bought her a house, cars, and anything else she wanted.

Nicole got out of the shower naked and walked into her room, looking in the mirror.

"Damn, I look better than Beyoncé," she said.

Nicole turning up her stereo, blasting Keith Sweat while rubbing lotion on her soft legs. She put on some pink boy shorts with no panties, and a t-shirt that said "Fuck It." Nicole played with her wet tight pussy every morning, unless Killer was in town, because he would fuck her brains out. Nicole know it was wrong to have sex with her nephew. She even slipped up and got pregnant a while back, but she got rid of the baby. The dick was amazing to her, though. Nicole thought about sucking his dick and got wetter. Then she heard her doorbell ringing.

She made her way downstairs, hoping it wasn't Pudd, a young man that was an upcoming rapper who lived a couple houses down. Ever since she gave him some sweet pussy, he'd been stalking a bitch.

The crazy part was that all Pudd did was eat her pussy. then she always kicked him out.

Nicole opened the door, talking shit as if she already knew who it was.

"Nigga, stop coming to my fucking house before-" She stopped midsentence when she realized the two men standing at her door weren't Pudd.

"I'm sorry. May I help you?" Nicole said, eyeing the men with her hazel eyes, impressed with the handsome man in the Muslim garment with the neat dreads. He was just how she liked her men, chocolate and sexy.

"Good morning," Savage said, putting a gun in her face, causing her to go back inside her house speechless.

Big Art closed the door behind them, pulling out his pistol and looking around to see pictures of her and Killer everywhere.

"I'll check the house," Big Art said as he went to search the house.

"I haven't seen him in years," Nicole said with tears.

"Listen, I am giving you a chance, pretty lady, but please don't test me," Savage said.

"I swear to Jesus, I don't know where he is," Nicole said.

"Let me tell you a story before I kill you," Savage said, pulling up a chair between her legs, making her wetter.

"Killer fucked up my life. He killed my mom, Lisa, my homies, and almost killed my baby brother," Savage said.

Nicole heard the name Lisa and her mind shifted form 0-100.

"Oh my God, you look like him," Nicole said, covering her mouth in shock.

Savage looked at her with a confused expression as Big Art walked up to tell him the house was clear.

"You're Lisa Braxton's son," Nicole said, wiping her tears.

"He told you that?" Savage said, getting pissed.

"No, please listen. I can explain. Go look in my bedroom by my dresser, on the third shelf the pictures, and it will explain it all," Nicole said, shaking.

"If you're playing any type of games, I am blowing your fucking brains out. Art watch this bitch," Savage said as he walked upstairs.

After he grabbed a stack of photos, he came back downstairs.

"What is this?" Savage asked.

"Read the letter," Nicole said.

The letter read...

If anything ever happens, please take care of my child, sis. Please. He has a brother out there in Florida, I believe. His mother is Lisa Braxton. But please take care of my son. His father, Tone, left with my heart and now the drugs took my soul. I feel death.

Jessica Luv U

Savage's head was spinning. *How could this be*, he thought.

"Here are pics of your father and Jessica," said Nicole.

When Savage saw the pics, he realized it was really him, Tone, his father. Then he saw pics of a woman and him, must have been Jessica. His mother told him about her dirty ex friend. He also saw a pic of Killer as a child, and they looked like twins as kids.

"This is crazy," Savage said.

"Killer's real name is Tone Jr.," said Nicole.

"I have been holding the secret for years, but I had no idea the "Savage" person was you, and I'm sorry for all your losses, but he is your brother," Nicole said.

"I don't know what I can do after-" Savage was interrupted before he finished his sentence.

Boom. Boom. Boom. Boom was all Savage heard as Art shot Nicole in her head.

"What the fuck wrong with you?" Savage asked him.

"They killed my unborn and you talking about a family reunion. they almost killed you. It's a life for a life," Art said, walking out the house with an attitude.

Savage took all the pics, and letter, and made his way out the door, confused as to how to handle this now, since he was out to kill his brother and family.

Chapter 26
JoJo Back

JoJo had been in Mexico for the past couple of years, laying low to build his own empire, with the help of a new cartel family. He'd retired years ago, just to get off the FBI's radar. He was now the biggest supplier in Mexico. JoJo had also been supplying Montana before his murder. Montana still owed him 9 million dollars, and somebody had to pay it.

JoJo only had one roadblock from taking over North America, as well, and that was Umer's empire. He hated that African piece of shit.

JoJo had used Savage as a pawn to kill all of his competitors. It was part of the game. JoJo was on his private jet, flying to Miami to prepare for his meeting with Flaco and Killer. He had plans to eliminate Savage, then Flaco and Killer would be next before he took over. Britt was a strong girl. He knew she'd be ok. She knew it was a cold game

***

Khadija was in her dodge truck on her laptop, looking at the pictures of her next victim, and reading the location. This hit was special, not because it was worth 5 million, but because it was requested by her father.

Khadija morally sent the money to charities, or to her brother to open up schools and camps to train his Zulu army.

Khadija walked in her secret apartment, which nobody knew anything about because it was a secret location filled with guns, a gym, and snakes.

***

Umer was swimming in his huge pool in his Africa mansion, with over eighty guards surrounding the mansion, ready to kill. After his daily swim, he got dressed and prepared for the rest of his day.

"Sir, your daughter has confirmed your message," said his assistant.

"Thank you," Umer said with a smile, hoping she would complete it. If not, then she would die at his request.

***

Brit and Savage were out shopping when JoJo called.

"Hey, sis. What ya doing?" JoJo asked.

"Just doing some shopping with my husband for my birthday coming soon," Britt said.

"Okay, I have something special for you. Did you speak to Mice?" JoJo asked.

"Yeah," she said sadly.

"Put Savage on," JoJo requested.

Britt handed him the phone while walking into a Hermes store.

"My man, Savage, long time no speak," JoJo said.

"Same here, I'm good. How are you?" Savage asked. I got some important info for you. I need to see you in private. I am sending you an address and time," JoJo said, sounding sincere.

"Okay, anything for you, bro. You're the reason I am where I'm at," Savage said.

"Okay," JoJo said before hanging up.

Savage passed Britt her phone while she shopped for the both of them. Savage wondered what did JoJo had to tell him. He had a feeling it was about Goya's murder, who was his old friend.

***

Hours later…

Savage threw on his bulletproof vest, as he had been doing lately. It was better to be safe than sorry. Savage put two pistols with extended clips in his side hostlers, preparing to leave for this meeting.

"I am going to meet JoJo, boo," Savage announced.

"Okay, here go the address. See you later," Britt said, passing him a piece of paper.

Savage pulled off in one of his Hummers as two others followed him full of security guards. Savage realized the address was a warehouse. Something didn't feel right, he thought.

JoJo had a twenty men security team surrounding the warehouse while he sat at a table by himself, wearing a Brook Brothers suit. JoJo was twenty minutes early, something he always did for security reasons, and respect. JoJo sat at the round table, smoking a cigar, hoping his everything would go as planned. He was going to speak to Savage while Flaco and Killer ambushed them, and killed Savage. Meanwhile, his security team was instructed to take out whatever men Savage had arrived with.

He'd already come up with a story to tell his sister, and he was sure she'd buy it. JoJo saw a couple of his men walking the top tier to patrol the area as they did every four minutes.

Seconds later, JoJo saw his men flying over the rail to the ground, dropping like bags. JoJo hid under the table, wondering what the fuck was going on.

JoJo looked everywhere for the killers, but no one was in sight. He waited for the rest of his team to come, just in case he got shot, and he was gunless.

JoJo saw a black shadow spring like lighting across the top tier, and then jump down a flight of stairs.

Khadija had been waiting there for over an hour. She didn't even break a sweat killing all of his men outside with her silencer, one by one.

Khadija walked towards JoJo slowly, as if she was on a runway. When she saw him hiding, she laughed.

"So all American men are pussies," Khadija said in a strong Africa accent.

"You can come out. I killed your team outside," she said softly, holding a gun with a silencer on it.

JoJo came from under the table to see a woman dressed in all black with a ski mask that only showed her grey eyes. JoJo admired her coca-cola bottle shaped body.

"What the fuck are you?" JoJo said nervously.

"It doesn't matter," Khadjia said.

"I can pay you double, or triple. Please," JoJo said.

"No, thank you. The king of Africa sent me. I'm his daughter, the Snake of Death," Khadija said.

JoJo had heard of the Snake of Death. He thought it was a myth, or a legend. The name rang bells all over the world because of brutal murders, where snakes were left to eat the rest of the dead bodies.

Khadija shot him over seven times and then he pulled out a black snake from her book bag and laid it on JoJo's dead body.

Khadija made her way back up to the roof to exit, as if she was Bat Woman.

Chapter 27
Should I

Savage and his men arrived at the warehouse just on time, but there was a funny vibe about the warehouse with two vans parked in the front.

"Yo, boss, this nigga ain't got security?" Big Lo asked.

"Shit, guess not," Savage said as he got out of his truck with his team behind him. Savage saw a leg poking out from under a tree log, so he pulled out his gun. As he and his men got closer, they saw four dead Mexicans lying in the bushes behind a fence.

Savage made his way into the warehouse to see dead bodies everywhere, all Mexicans. Then he saw a familiar face laying on the side of a table.

"What the fuck?" Savage said as he pulled the table to the side to see JoJo's face and body. It looked as if an animal had chewed at his flesh.

"Boss, watch out. It's a snake," Big Lo said as he shot the snake dead in its place to keep it from attacking his boss.

"We gotta get outta here now," Savage said, stepping over dead bodies.

As soon as they stepped outside, they were ambushed with bullets from high power guns. Savage saw a Mexican running from tree to tree behind the fence, busting. Savage pulled out and shot towards the trees while ducking. About six men were already dead. The rest took cover while firing in they're direction.

Flaco and Killer had arrived two minutes after Savage and his crew. When they saw dead bodies and the hummers, they figured JoJo's plan had backfired, so they hid in the bushes.

Killer saw Savage was out of bullets, so when he tried to reload, Killer shot the guard to the left of him in his heart.

Then he shot Savage in the arm as he tried to run while shooting.

Savage and Big R were the last men standing, and were both out of bullets, so they weighed their options. Then they ran and jumped in the hummer, pulling off while bullets rained on the bulletproof truck.

Killer and Flaco ran down the street to hop in the Benz. Sirens could be heard a block away so they went the opposite way.

Savage told Big R to take him to the Dr. Ali Akbar's house in South Miami have his wound examined. Dr. Ali was the household doctor for criminals and poor people without healthcare.

Savage was confused as to why and how Flaco and Killer followed them and was able to get a heads up on him, unless it was a setup that went wrong, Savage thought

Meka was laying in the hospital bed in labor, sweating and squeezing the life out of Big Art's hand.

"Come on, baby. Push. You can do it," Art said.

"Miss, you have to push harder or you will hurt the baby," the doctor said, hoping she would push harder.

"I'm tired, fuckkk," Meka yelled, pushing extra harder so her child would come out.

"Yes, the head is out. Keep pushing," the doc said.

About two minutes later, a beautiful baby boy came out, weighing 7 ½ pounds. Big Art had tears in his eyes. After the nurses cleansed the blood, Big Art cut the cord, and the child was taken for tests.

"I'm so happy. Now we got a real family. I hope you can leave the streets alone and stop acting so odd," Meka said.

"Baby, let's just enjoy our son," Big Art said as the doctor came in with a serious look on his face.

"I am sorry but we're going to need to keep the infant for a couple of days because it seems as if he has a virus and his white blood cells are fighting it."

Big Art looked at the doctor as if he was speaking French or Chinese. He spoke Creole, but it wasn't foreign.

"Okay," Meka said nervously.

Big Art looked worried, as if he saw the ghostbusters come into the room. He sat down.

The doctors left out the room looking at Art oddly because of his reaction to the news.

"Art, what the fuck is wrong with you? Lately, you been acting weird. It's freaking me out. We got too much going on. Are you high on PCP or crack?" Meka asked seriously.

"Meka, I have something to tell you that will break us, or we can be strong together. Please, just don't hate me," Art said as he stared out the window, unable to look her in her eyes.

Art knew Meka was the one he wanted to die with, and grow with. He couldn't live without her heart.

Meka sat there wondering why he made no eye contact. She had a feeling it was drugs he was on, which would explain his weight loss, lack of energy, and miserable ways.

"Meka, I was having affair with my assistant, Ms. Lee, before she died, and she was pregnant with my child," Art said slowly.

"How could you, after all we've been through? I was loyal to you. I never did you wrong," Meka said as tears rolled down her pretty face.

"I'm sorry, boo. It was me not being 100% loyal," Art said.

"I'm sure we can work it out, but this is a lot," Meka said.

"Meka, that is not the bad part," Art said.

Meka started to cry more because she thought it was more than one female. It was too good to be true.

"She gave me HIV," Art said as tears flowed down his chin.

Meka was so shocked she didn't even realize she was crying.

"I'm sorry," Art said.

Meka picked up the food tray, remote, and pillow, and threw them at Big Art because she had no strength to get up.

"I fucking hate you, bitch. Stay way from me and my son. I hope you die, you nasty dick nigga," Meka yelled as if she wanted the whole hospital to hear her.

Art made his way out the door, but before he, left he turned around.

"I am making it right and making your wish come true. Y'all don't need to worry about me again," Art said as he closed the door. He heard something hit it behind him and her yelling, "Fuck you and your diseased ass."

Chapter 28
Suicidal Thoughts

Britt had been home all day with Lil Smoke, praying and making Duwa (a form of worship).

Last night someone killed her brother, JoJo, before Savage arrived at their meeting. She felt as if her life had been snatched from under her feet. Britt loved her brother. He'd raised her and was always there for her.

Britt knew for a fact someone knew what happened at that warehouse. The news had reported "A well-known, rich business man was murdered with 33 others."

Brit loved and trusted her husband. He was the last person she'd point a finger at, but she did find it strange that he was the last person to see him alive. To make matters worse, he had a bullet wound, and explained how he'd gotten ambushed when he came out of the warehouse after seeing JoJo's dead body.

Britt turned on her phone to see she had a few missed calls, most of them from Meka. She'd left voicemails, one saying she had the baby, and the rest were her crying and not saying a word. Britt had her own issue. She felt like life wasn't worth living. She went to make Lil Smoke's lunch as she wiped her tears away.

***

Big Art hadn't been to sleep since he left the hospital. it felt as if Meka's words were lodged in his head. Big Art thought back to the days he was incarcerated in Pollack and Victorville USP telling himself there was more to life than drugs, money, and the fast life.

Art thought becoming a Muslim would change his life for the better, but he forgot about the tests Allah would throw at him.

Art picked up a pen and paper and wrote a letter.

Dear Meka, I'm sorry I brought pain to you and my son's lives. I never meant to. You really deserve better, and more than me. I fucked up. Please tell my son I love him, and I'm sorry. I love you. I hope we meet again in the hereafter of Allah Akbar.

Big Art laid the note on the dresser as he pulled out a 357 a shot himself in the head with a smile on his face.

***

Before Meka left the hospital, the doctor told her that she and her child both were HIV positive. She left the hospital in a cab with her child. The doctor gave her a lot of meds to give her son. She was advised that if she didn't, then Lil Author wouldn't make it past ten.

"Excuse me, sir, can you take me to Carroll City?" Meka asked the cab driver, handing him a twenty dollar bill.

"Okay, sure, and congratulations," the Haitian driver said, looking at the baby wrapped tightly in her arms.

"Thank you," Meka said coldly.

"Where is he father? I'm sure he is proud," the cab driver side while driving.

"Nigga, that's none of your fucking business. I paid you to drive, not talk," Meka yelled.

The driver shut up. He couldn't figure out how such a pretty lady was without the child's father.

The man drove in silence. Meka was in deep thought. She was heartbroken because she felt her baby didn't deserve to die nor be tortured with a disease. Meka loved Art, but she loved nobody enough to carry their disease. She felt hopeful, though. Since he had HIV, who would love her man?

Meka was on her way home to pack up some of her and Lil Author's shit so they could go.

Big Art never got a chance to sign the birth certificate. Meka was so mad that she'd just said things she didn't mean. Once they arrived home, she saw Art's truck parked out front. She got nervous and angry, but she made her way inside.

Meka laid her son in his room while he was asleep. As she packed some items, she prayed Art wouldn't come try to stop her because she wasn't staying. He'd given her and her son HIV, she could never forgive him for fucking their lives up.

Meka went to the closet to get her Gucci suitcase to pack her belongings, but she started to wonder where Art was. She disliked him, but she still loved him, even after everything that had happened.

"Art where are you? We have to talk," Meka said, walking into their bedroom. She froze at the door.

Meka screamed when she saw Art laying on the wooden floor with a bullet wound in his head and his gun in his hand.

Meka was crying a river of tears. She didn't even care about the HIV anymore. She just wanted Art to come back. Meka looked around to see if it was a setup, but when she saw the note on the dresser and read it, she fell to her knees, knowing it was her fault.

Meka called 911 and told them her husband killed himself. She heard her baby crying, so she went to get him. She wanted to pick the gun up and shoot herself, but she realized she had a son to raise.

Meka called Savage and told him what happened. He told her not to move. And the police showed up moments later.

Chapter 29
Flaco Date

Savage and Bama sat in the Mosque office in deep thought about the setup, Killer and Flaco, and even Big Art's death.

"Britt has been acting really funny lately," Savage said.

"Well you were the last person to see him alive, and you got hit, so you do the math," Bama said.

"Whoever killed JoJo gave him a couple of headshots and fed him to a snake. He must have got into it with a dangerous cartel," Savage said.

"Yeah, but a snake is unheard of," Bama said.

The men heard a little knock.

"Come in," Bama said.

Khadija walked in with a bright smile, looking amazing in her Gucci dress with her hair out. "As-salaam-alaikum," Khadija said to both men with her soft eyes and sweet soft voice.

"I have to go back home for a couple of days to handle some important things," she said to Bama, kissing his lips.

"Okay, my love. Be safe, and hurry back," Bama said.

"No worries about protection, I never missed yet. Oh yeah, I hope you feel better, Savage. I heard what happened. Maybe one day you should come to the shooting range with me," Khadija said as she walked out smiling and giving Savage a funny look.

"Damn, did you have to tell her? And it's really something about her that's off. I can feel it," Savage said.

"Listen, she is my wife. Give her a chance. You can't judge something you don't know. And I'm sure she can help you with your shooting. I heard she got the best shot in Africa," Bama said with a chuckle.

Savage thought about the letter Big Art left. He was hurt. His friend took his own life because of HIV. Savage had a feeling he was going through something, but not HIV, and to pass it to his wife and newborn son.

***

Britt let Meka stay in the guest house, which had 2 bed-rooms, 2 bathrooms, a kitchen, living room, and a dining area, until she got her life in order. They were friends and family.

Britt was at home in her living room watching "Cold Case" on TNT, thinking about JoJo. She had been ducking Savage lately because she wanted to figure out who killed her brother, and Savage was her main suspect as of now.

Britt went to check on Lil Smoke, who was playing his XBOX. Then she made her way to the guest house to check on Meka and her child.

When Britt walked into the guest house, she called Meka's name, but there was no answer. Britt checked every room, and found nothing. But once she opened the bathroom door, tears immediately began flowing down her face.

Meka laid in the corner of the bathroom with her wrists cut and blood everywhere. She was dead. Britt saw the little baby floating on his little stomach inside the tub, dead. His whole body was blue. Meka had drowned him.

Britt call the cleanup crew from her cell phone, and she got on her walkie-talkie and paged security. Then she saw a letter on the sink.

I'm sorry but I couldn't live my life like this, and see my son being HIV positive. I didn't want it to spread. We will see you one day.

Love Meka

Britt moved out of security's way. They were amazed to see the pretty woman and the baby dead.

***

The next morning, Khadija was ready for action, as always, because she was still in America. The trip to Africa was a lie to buy her some time to spy.

Flaco and Killer had been being watched ever since they left the warehouse shooting. they had no clue a black dodge truck followed them daily.

Khadija knew these two men were her husband's headache. She overheard him talk about them daily. After she killed JoJo, she saw the two pulling up, acting sneaky. So she watched them from the rooftop that night. She even saw when Savage got shot, and she laughed. She was going to do what Savage couldn't to relieve stress off of her husband, today was the day.

Khadija left her low key apartment geared up with an Africa black snake in her book bag as she hopped in her truck, heading towards Flaco's hideout.

It was four a.m. and Flaco was leaving his apartment to spy on Savage, hopeful to catch him slipping. Once downstairs, Flaco saw a beautiful woman dressed in an all-black dress with long hair, trying to get in the building.

Flaco thought she must have forgotten her keys, but it looked as if she'd just come back from a club or a sleepover, because of her Gucci book bag.

When Flaco got closer, he saw her pretty feet in her red bottom shoes, perfect breasts, and her eyes were exotic. He had to have her.

"Good morning, beautiful. I'm pretty sure you are waiting for your man or just coming from being with him, but I would love to take you out sometime," Flaco said, standing face to face with the beauty.

"I'm sorry, I'm married," Khadija said as she pulled out a blade swiftly and quickly. He didn't even see it coming until he was on the floor, holding his neck and taking his last breath. Khadija pulled out a long snake and threw it on his face. As the snake finished the job, she walked off with her high heels clicking against the concrete.

Chapter 30
Visa Sohaje

Days Later

A federal agent had just left Savage's house a couple of minutes ago, informing Britt that JoJo's murder case was going cold. The agent informed her that they'd found a lot of shell cases outside, but JoJo was shot with a .357, which left no shells. He instructed her to give him a call ASAP if she heard anything, as he walked out.

Once he left, Britt started to cry like a baby. She knew for a fact Savage and his crew were the only team to use 357 guns to leave a trade sign. Britt grabbed her duffle bag from the closet, went to kiss Lil Smoke, and told the guards to take care of Lil Smoke as she rushed out.

***

Khadija was in the house, cleaning as she normally did, hoping to be a good housewife.

"Hi, baby, how was your trip?" Bama said as he walked into the kitchen.

"Huh,'" she said, forgetting she told him she'd gone to Africa.

"Oh yeah, good. It's always good to go back to the motherland," she said, like a true African.

"My father said my brother hopes to meet you soon," she added.

"That's great, but I missed you. And I'm a little relived. One of the guys we been hunting was found dead from stab wounds and a poisonous snake, the same shit from JoJo's murder. Somebody is trying to send us a message, or to hell," Bama said in deep thought.

"Be safe, baby, and maybe you should focus on our life and starting our own family," Khadija said with a warm smile.

"Yeah, you right. We will talk about that later. Now finish cleaning and come to the Mosque," Bama said as he left his house.

***

Savage drove to the graveyard to see his mother's grave. It was the anniversary of her death. Savage felt as if it was all his fault that his friends and family were dead.

Savage had a bottle of Henny with him in his passenger seat and two 357s, pulling up to the graveyard.

When he went to his mother's grave, he felt like his life was at a dead end. As he took a sip from the bottle, tears poured down his face and the dark clouds started to come together over his head.

"Mom, I'm sorry. I'm done with this life. I am taking care of Lil Smoke and being a good husband. I deserve to give my family that," Savage said as he poured out some Henny on his mother and Rich's graves. Rich was buried right next to her.

Savage thought he heard footsteps, but when he reached for his guns on his hips, he realized he'd left them in his Benz.

"I'm glad you made it. I've been waiting today. It was the day I killed her sexy ass. Remember?" Killer said, pointing a gun four feet behind him.

"Just to get back at me," Savage said as he took a sip of Henny. He turned around to look in Killer's eyes.

"You destroyed my empires," Killer said.

"You should never go up against a savage. But before you kill me, I think you should know your my blood brother," Savage said with a serious face.

"That's not gonna save you," Killer said laughing.

"Our father's name is Tone. He was murdered 2/10/1990, the day I was born. Your mother was Jessica, my mother, Lisa's, best friend." Killer lowered his gun because he knew the story just as well. Tears came down Savage's face as he told the rest of the story.

As soon as they were about to embrace, Killer's head was blown off his shoulders, splashing blood all over Savage. He picked up Killer's pistol and aimed it at the shooter, who had the gun aimed at him with a crazy look in her eyes.

"What the fuck wrong with you? Put the gun down, Britt," said Savage, as they stod there, aiming their guns at each other.

"That was my brother," savage said sternly.

"Good. Now we almost even, bitch," Britt said with an evil stare.

"What? I didn't kill JoJo. Believe me. Put the gun down, please. I love you," Savage said.

"Oh yeah, just like you loved Jada. Yeah, I killed that bitch, Randall. I saw you was creeping to hotels. You loved her, too," Britt said through tears.

"I'm sorry, Britt. It was a mistake. I gave my life to you," Savage said with tears flowing down his face.

Britt wanted to pull the trigger so badly, but she couldn't do it. His words were so sincere to her as she lowered her 357.

Britt walked over towards him, but bullets came from nowhere, ripping her body apart. Her last words were, "love you," as she fell in front of his feet.

Once Savage saw she was gone, he saw Bama standing in front of him.

"I thought she was about to kill you," Bama said.

Savage aimed his gun at Bama, while he aimed his gun back.

"What the fuck?" Bama said.

"You killed my wife. It's a life for a life," Savage said.

"You are trying to kill me over a bitch," Bama said with a chuckle.

Savage shot him in his shoulder but then, out of the left corner, Khadija came busting bullets form a high powered gun, hitting Savage over ten times in his chest.

"You saved my life, baby. How did you know I was here?" Bama asked, rubbing his wound.

"I followed you," Khadija said as she went into her book bag to pull out a snake. Then she threw it on Savage's body.

Bama was confused, but he'd talk to her later, he thought to himself.

"We gotta get to a hospital or Dr. Ali ASAP, baby," Bama said, in pain, trying not to move.

"I don't think you will make it," Khadija said in a soft voice as she disarmed him and roundhouse kicked him, making him fall.

"Big Zoe paid me years ago to kill your crew, and I always complete my mission, baby. But I did and do love you, baby. I promise my love for you is real. I'll see you," Khadija said as she let off six shot in his chest while crying.

As soon as she turned around, she saw SWAT trucks and FBI coats with guns out screaming "Freeze."

Khadija smiled, and got on one knee, acting as if she was about to surrender, but instead she let off shots from her assault rifle, killing four agents before they started to shoot as she ran off into the woods without a trace.

To Be Continued…
Life of a Savage 4
Coming Soon

Submission Guideline

Submit the first three chapters of your completed manuscript to ldpsubmissions@gmail.com, subject line: Your book's title. The manuscript must be in a .doc file and sent as an attachment. Document should be in Times New Roman, double spaced and in size 12 font. Also, provide your synopsis and full contact information. If sending multiple submissions, they must each be in a separate email.

Have a story but no way to send it electronically? You can still submit to LDP/Ca$h Presents. Send in the first three chapters, written or typed, of your completed manuscript to:

LDP: Submissions Dept
Po Box 944
Stockbridge, Ga 30281

DO NOT send original manuscript. Must be a duplicate.

Provide your synopsis and a cover letter containing your full contact information.

Thanks for considering LDP and Ca$h Presents.

BAE BELONGS TO ME III

A DOPE BOY'S QUEEN II

By **Aryanna**

CHAINED TO THE STREETS III

By **J-Blunt**

COKE KINGS V

KING OF THE TRAP II

By **T.J. Edwards**

GORILLAZ IN THE BAY V

TEARS OF A GANGSTA II

De'Kari

THE STREETS ARE CALLING II

Duquie Wilson

KINGPIN KILLAZ IV

STREET KINGS III

PAID IN BLOOD III

CARTEL KILLAZ IV

DOPE GODS II

Hood Rich

SINS OF A HUSTLA II

ASAD

TRIGGADALE III

Elijah R. Freeman

KINGZ OF THE GAME V

Playa Ray

SLAUGHTER GANG IV

RUTHLESS HEART IV

By Willie Slaughter

THE HEART OF A SAVAGE III

By Jibril Williams

FUK SHYT II

By Blakk Diamond

THE REALEST KILLAS

By Tranay Adams

TRAP GOD II

By Troublesome

YAYO III

A SHOOTER'S AMBITION III

By S. Allen

GHOST MOB

Stilloan Robinson

KINGPIN DREAMS III

By Paper Boi Rari

CREAM

By Yolanda Moore

SON OF A DOPE FIEND II

By Renta

FOREVER GANGSTA II

GLOCKS ON SATIN SHEETS II

By Adrian Dulan

LOYALTY AIN'T PROMISED II

By Keith Williams

THE PRICE YOU PAY FOR LOVE II

DOPE GIRL MAGIC III

By Destiny Skai

CONFESSIONS OF A GANGSTA II

By Nicholas Lock

I'M NOTHING WITHOUT HIS LOVE II

By Monet Dragun

CAUGHT UP IN THE LIFE III

By Robert Baptiste

NEW TO THE GAME III

By **Malik D. Rice**

LIFE OF A SAVAGE IV

By **Romell Tukes**

QUIET MONEY II

By **Trai'Quan**

THE STREETS MADE ME II

By **Larry D. Wright**

THE ULTIMATE SACRIFICE VI

IF YOU CROSSM ME ONCE II

By **Anthony Fields**

THE LIFE OF A HOOD STAR

By Ca$h & Rashia Wilson

<u>**Available Now**</u>

RESTRAINING ORDER **I & II**

By **CA$H & Coffee**

LOVE KNOWS NO BOUNDARIES **I II & III**

By **Coffee**

RAISED AS A GOON I, II, III & IV

BRED BY THE SLUMS I, II, III

BLAST FOR ME I & II

ROTTEN TO THE CORE I II III

A BRONX TALE I, II, III

DUFFEL BAG CARTEL I II III IV

HEARTLESS GOON I II III IV

A SAVAGE DOPEBOY I II

HEARTLESS GOON I II III

DRUG LORDS I II III

CUTTHROAT MAFIA

By **Ghost**

LAY IT DOWN **I & II**

LAST OF A DYING BREED

BLOOD STAINS OF A SHOTTA I & II III

By **Jamaica**

LOYAL TO THE GAME I II III

LIFE OF SIN I, II III

By **TJ & Jelissa**

BLOODY COMMAS I & II

SKI MASK CARTEL I II & III

KING OF NEW YORK I II,III IV V

RISE TO POWER I II III

COKE KINGS I II III IV

BORN HEARTLESS I II III IV

KING OF THE TRAP

By **T.J. Edwards**

IF LOVING HIM IS WRONG…I & II

LOVE ME EVEN WHEN IT HURTS I II III

By **Jelissa**

WHEN THE STREETS CLAP BACK I & II III

THE HEART OF A SAVAGE I II

By **Jibril Williams**

A DISTINGUISHED THUG STOLE MY HEART I II & III

LOVE SHOULDN'T HURT I II III IV

RENEGADE BOYS I II III IV

PAID IN KARMA I II III

By **Meesha**

A GANGSTER'S CODE I &, II III

A GANGSTER'S SYN I II III

THE SAVAGE LIFE I II III

CHAINED TO THE STREETS I II

By J-Blunt

PUSH IT TO THE LIMIT

By **Bre' Hayes**

BLOOD OF A BOSS **I, II, III, IV, V**

SHADOWS OF THE GAME

By **Askari**

THE STREETS BLEED MURDER **I, II & III**

THE HEART OF A GANGSTA I II& III

By **Jerry Jackson**

CUM FOR ME I II III IV V

An **LDP Erotica Collaboration**

BRIDE OF A HUSTLA **I II & II**

THE FETTI GIRLS **I, II& III**

CORRUPTED BY A GANGSTA I, II III, IV

BLINDED BY HIS LOVE

THE PRICE YOU PAY FOR LOVE

DOPE GIRL MAGIC I II

By **Destiny Skai**

WHEN A GOOD GIRL GOES BAD

By **Adrienne**

THE COST OF LOYALTY I II III

By Kweli

A GANGSTER'S REVENGE **I II III & IV**

THE BOSS MAN'S DAUGHTERS I II III IV V

A SAVAGE LOVE **I & II**

BAE BELONGS TO ME I II

A HUSTLER'S DECEIT I, II, III

WHAT BAD BITCHES DO I, II, III

SOUL OF A MONSTER I II III

KILL ZONE

A DOPE BOY'S QUEEN

By **Aryanna**

A KINGPIN'S AMBITON

A KINGPIN'S AMBITION **II**

I MURDER FOR THE DOUGH

By **Ambitious**

TRUE SAVAGE I II III IV V VI

Romell Tukes

DOPE BOY MAGIC I, II, III

MIDNIGHT CARTEL I II

By **Chris Green**

A DOPEBOY'S PRAYER

By **Eddie "Wolf" Lee**

THE KING CARTEL **I, II & III**

By **Frank Gresham**

THESE NIGGAS AIN'T LOYAL **I, II & III**

By **Nikki Tee**

GANGSTA SHYT **I II &III**

By **CATO**

THE ULTIMATE BETRAYAL

By **Phoenix**

BOSS'N UP **I , II & III**

By **Royal Nicole**

I LOVE YOU TO DEATH

By Destiny J

I RIDE FOR MY HITTA

I STILL RIDE FOR MY HITTA

By **Misty Holt**

LOVE & CHASIN' PAPER

By **Qay Crockett**

TO DIE IN VAIN

SINS OF A HUSTLA

By **ASAD**

BROOKLYN HUSTLAZ

By **Boogsy Morina**

BROOKLYN ON LOCK I & II

By **Sonovia**

GANGSTA CITY

By **Teddy Duke**

A DRUG KING AND HIS DIAMOND I & II III

A DOPEMAN'S RICHES

HER MAN, MINE'S TOO I, II

CASH MONEY HO'S

By Nicole Goosby

TRAPHOUSE KING **I II & III**

KINGPIN KILLAZ I II III

STREET KINGS I II

PAID IN BLOOD **I II**

CARTEL KILLAZ I II III

DOPE GODS

By **Hood Rich**

LIPSTICK KILLAH **I, II, III**

CRIME OF PASSION I II & III

By **Mimi**

STEADY MOBBN' **I, II, III**

THE STREETS STAINED MY SOUL

By **Marcellus Allen**

WHO SHOT YA **I, II, III**

SON OF A DOPE FIEND

Renta

GORILLAZ IN THE BAY **I II III IV**

TEARS OF A GANGSTA

DE'KARI

TRIGGADALE I II

Elijah R. Freeman

GOD BLESS THE TRAPPERS I, II, III

THESE SCANDALOUS STREETS I, II, III

FEAR MY GANGSTA I, II, III

THESE STREETS DON'T LOVE NOBODY I, II

BURY ME A G I, II, III, IV, V

A GANGSTA'S EMPIRE I, II, III, IV

THE DOPEMAN'S BODYGAURD I II

Tranay Adams

THE STREETS ARE CALLING

Duquie Wilson

MARRIED TO A BOSS... I II III

By Destiny Skai & Chris Green

KINGZ OF THE GAME I II III IV

Playa Ray

SLAUGHTER GANG I II III

RUTHLESS HEART I II III

By Willie Slaughter

FUK SHYT

By Blakk Diamond

DON'T F#CK WITH MY HEART I II

By Linnea

ADDICTED TO THE DRAMA I II III

By Jamila

YAYO I II

A SHOOTER'S AMBITION I II

By S. Allen

TRAP GOD

By Troublesome

FOREVER GANGSTA

GLOCKS ON SATIN SHEETS

By Adrian Dulan

TOE TAGZ I II III

By Ah'Million

KINGPIN DREAMS I II

By Paper Boi Rari

CONFESSIONS OF A GANGSTA

By Nicholas Lock

I'M NOTHING WITHOUT HIS LOVE

By Monet Dragun

CAUGHT UP IN THE LIFE I II

By Robert Baptiste

NEW TO THE GAME I II

By **Malik D. Rice**

LIFE OF A SAVAGE I II III

By **Romell Tukes**

LOYALTY AIN'T PROMISED

By Keith Williams

Quiet Money

By **Trai'Quan**

THE STREETS MADE ME

By **Larry D. Wright**

THE ULTIMATE SACRIFICE I, II, III, IV, V

KHADIFI

IF YOU CROSS ME ONCE

By **Anthony Fields**

THE LIFE OF A HOOD STAR

By Ca$h & Rashia Wilson

BOOKS BY LDP'S CEO, CA$H

TRUST IN NO MAN

TRUST IN NO MAN 2

TRUST IN NO MAN 3

BONDED BY BLOOD

SHORTY GOT A THUG

THUGS CRY

THUGS CRY 2

THUGS CRY 3

TRUST NO BITCH

TRUST NO BITCH 2

TRUST NO BITCH 3

TIL MY CASKET DROPS

RESTRAINING ORDER

RESTRAINING ORDER 2

IN LOVE WITH A CONVICT

LIFE OF A HOOD STAR

Coming Soon

BONDED BY BLOOD 2

BOW DOWN TO MY GANGSTA